Regina Public Library
BOOK SALE ITEM
~~ble
D0470168

RED RIVER RESISTANCE

A Girl Called ECHO

VOL. 2

By Katherena Vermette
Illustrated by Scott B. Henderson
Coloured by Donovan Yaciuk

HIGHWATER
PRESS

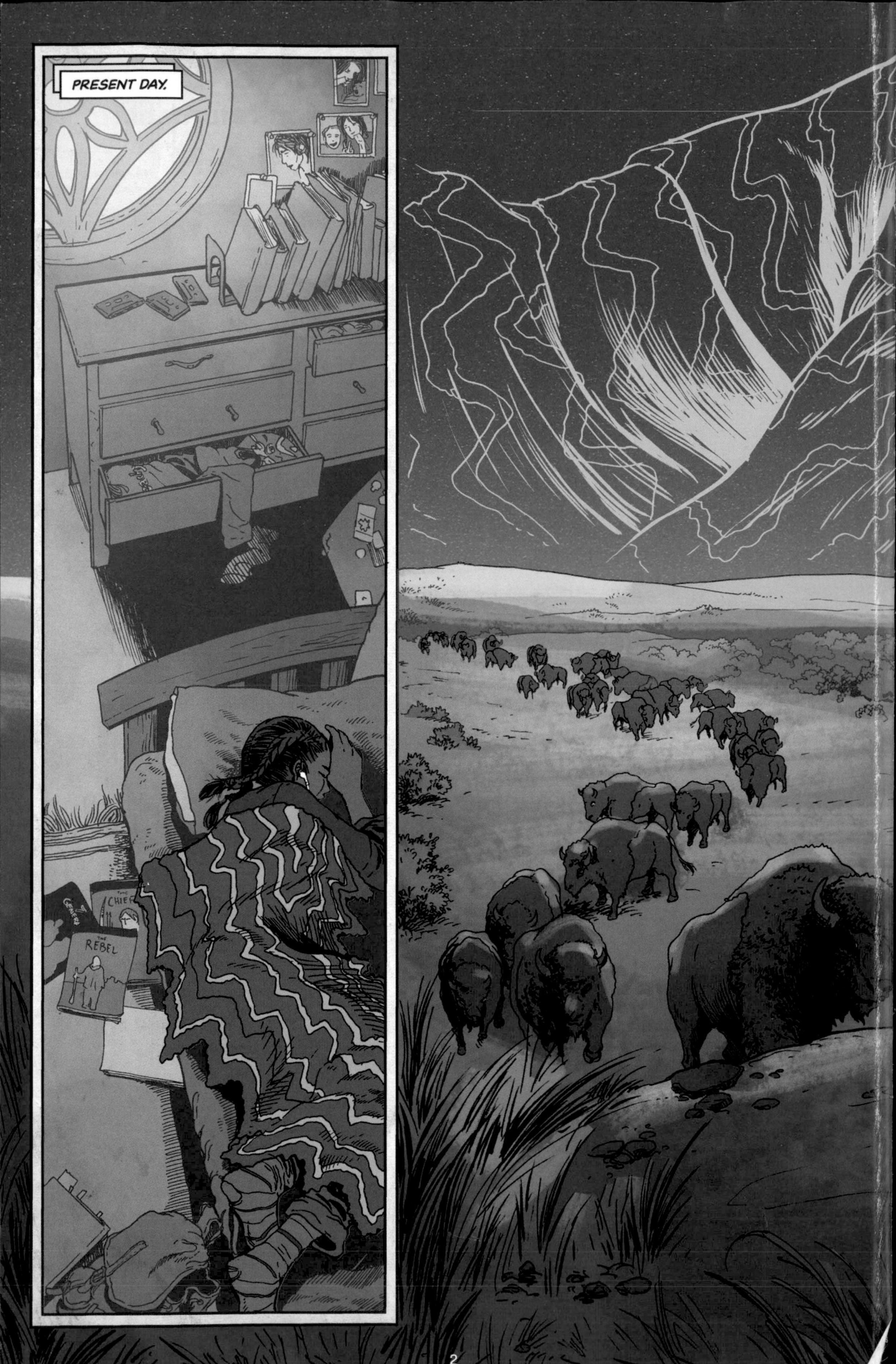
PRESENT DAY.
THE CHIEF
THE REBEL

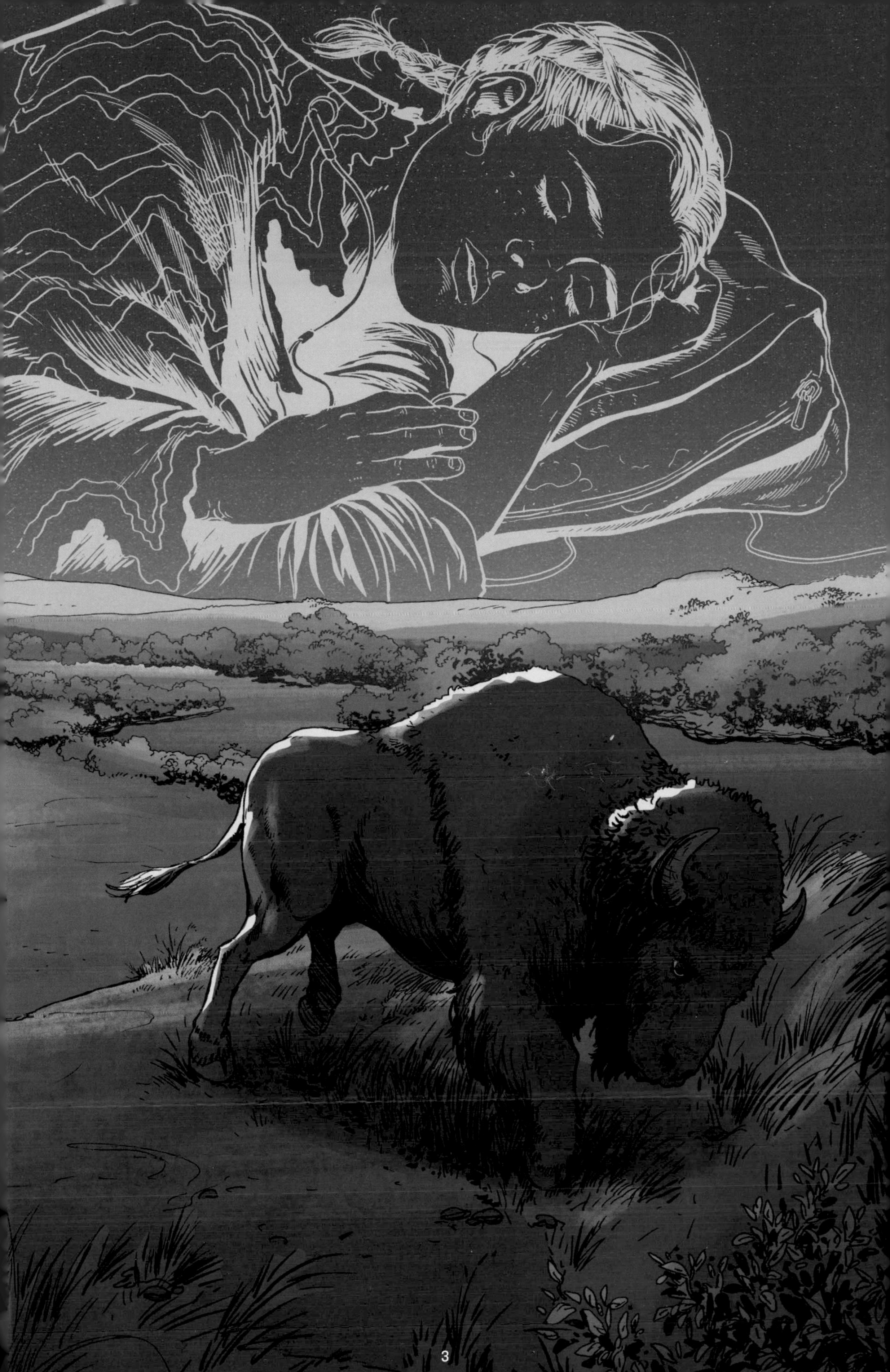

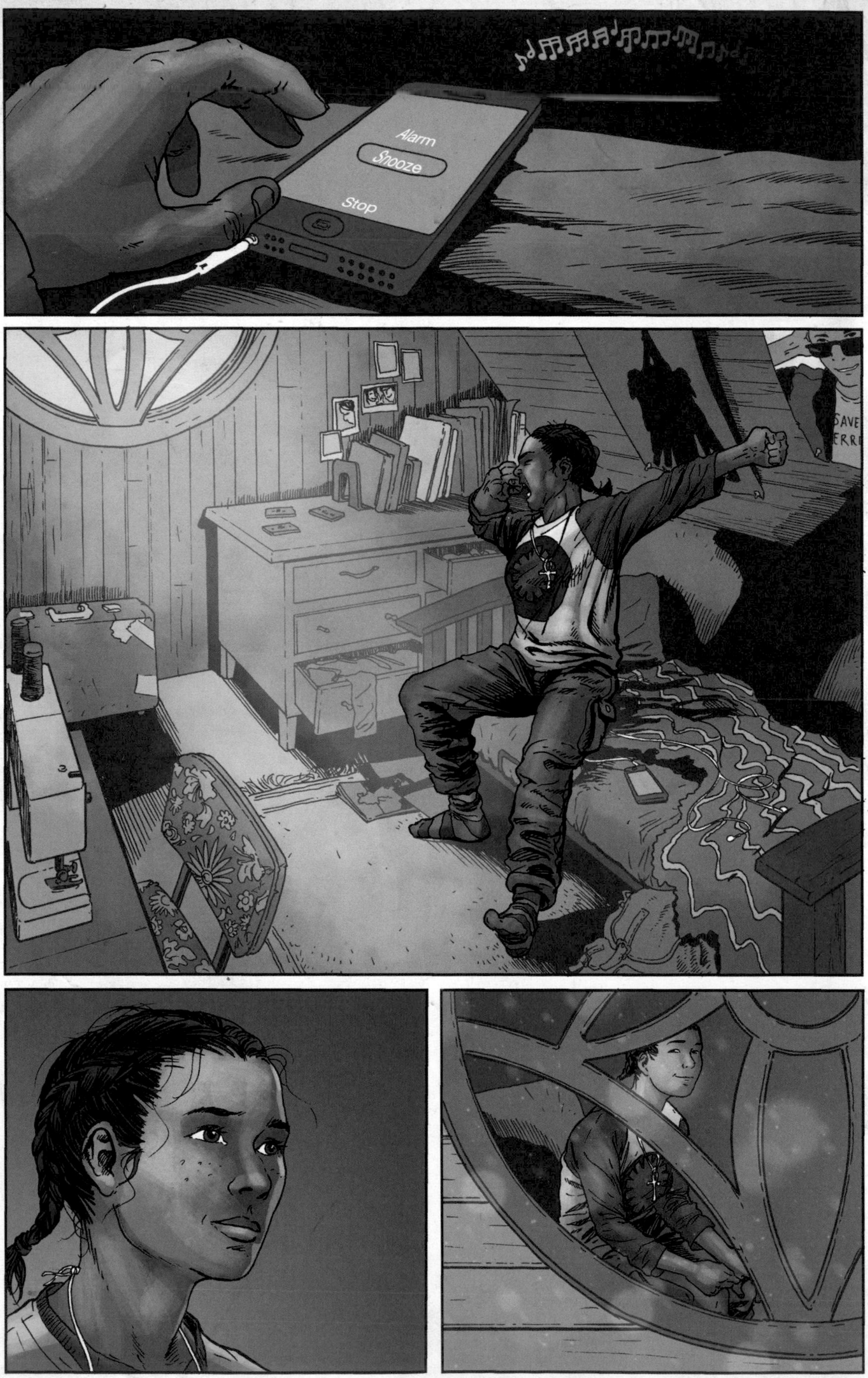
Alarm
Snooze
Stop

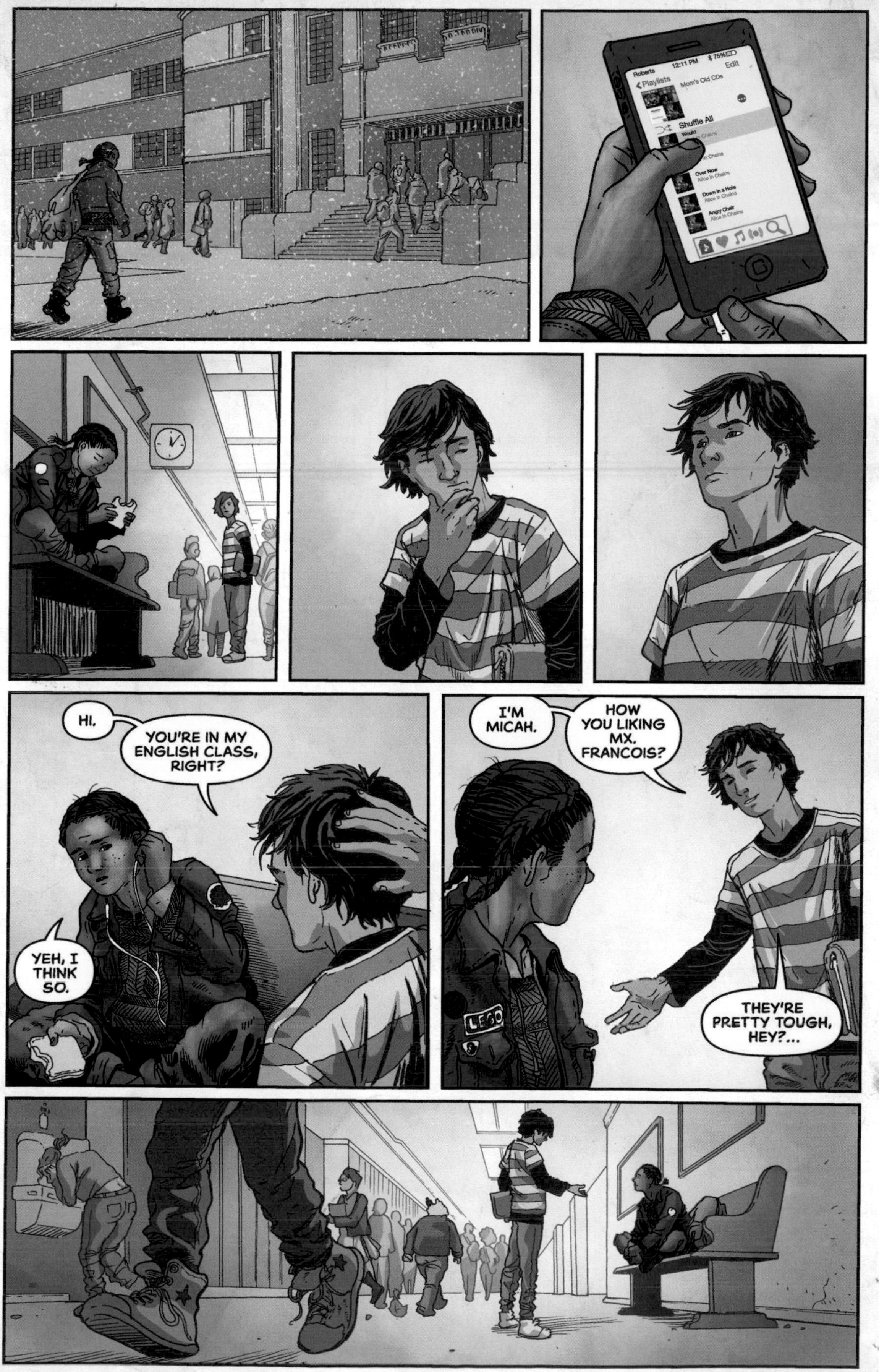

Roberts
12:11 PM
75%
Edit
Playlists
Mom's Old CDs
Shuffle All
Over Now
Alice In Chains
Down In a Hole
Alice In Chains
Angry Chair
Alice In Chains
HI.
YOU'RE IN MY ENGLISH CLASS, RIGHT?
YEH, I THINK SO.
I'M MICAH.
HOW YOU LIKING MX. FRANCOIS?
THEY'RE PRETTY TOUGH, HEY?...
LEGO

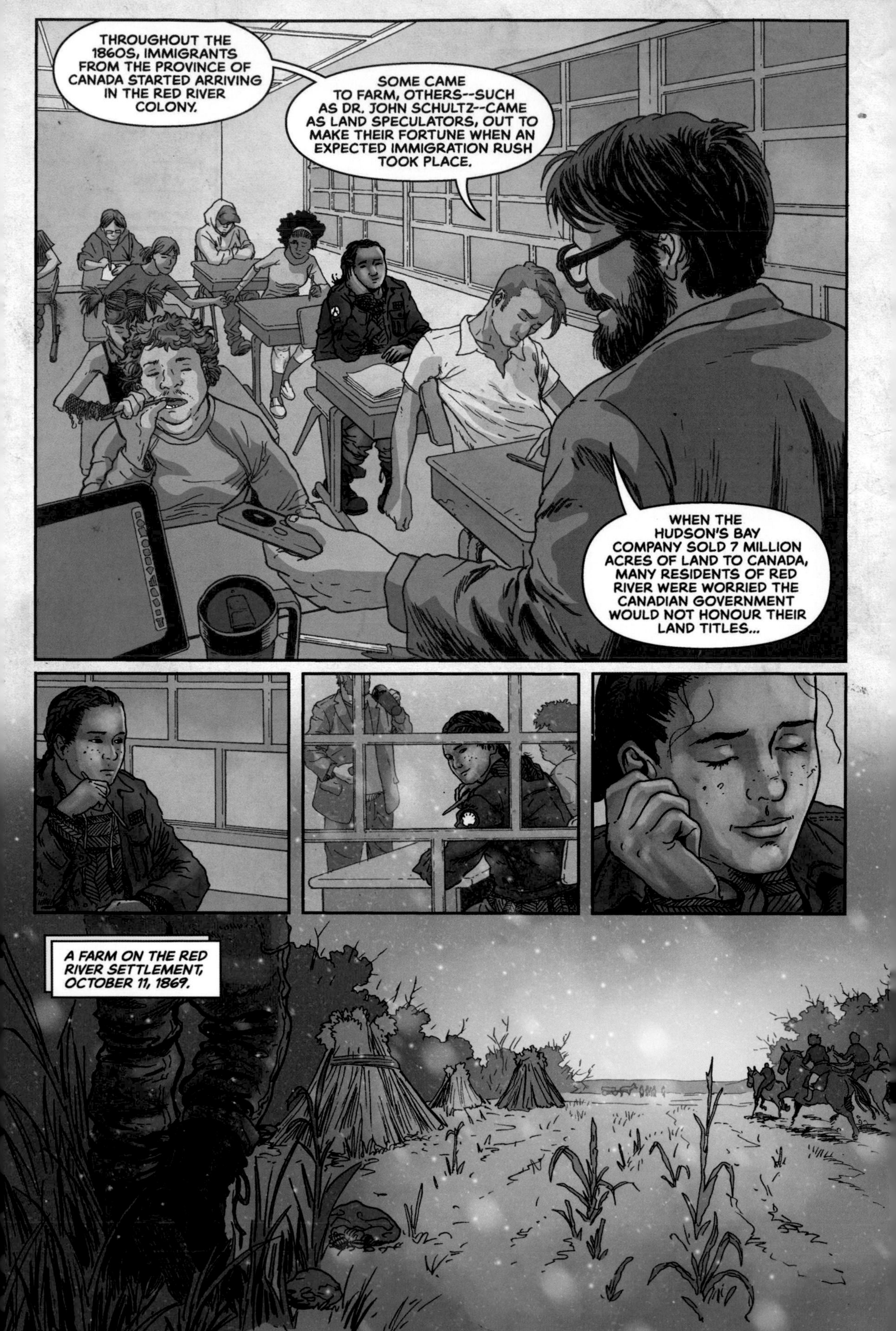
THROUGHOUT THE 1860S, IMMIGRANTS FROM THE PROVINCE OF CANADA STARTED ARRIVING IN THE RED RIVER COLONY.
SOME CAME TO FARM, OTHERS--SUCH AS DR. JOHN SCHULTZ--CAME AS LAND SPECULATORS, OUT TO MAKE THEIR FORTUNE WHEN AN EXPECTED IMMIGRATION RUSH TOOK PLACE.
WHEN THE HUDSON'S BAY COMPANY SOLD 7 MILLION ACRES OF LAND TO CANADA, MANY RESIDENTS OF RED RIVER WERE WORRIED THE CANADIAN GOVERNMENT WOULD NOT HONOUR THEIR LAND TITLES...
A FARM ON THE RED RIVER SETTLEMENT, OCTOBER 11, 1869.

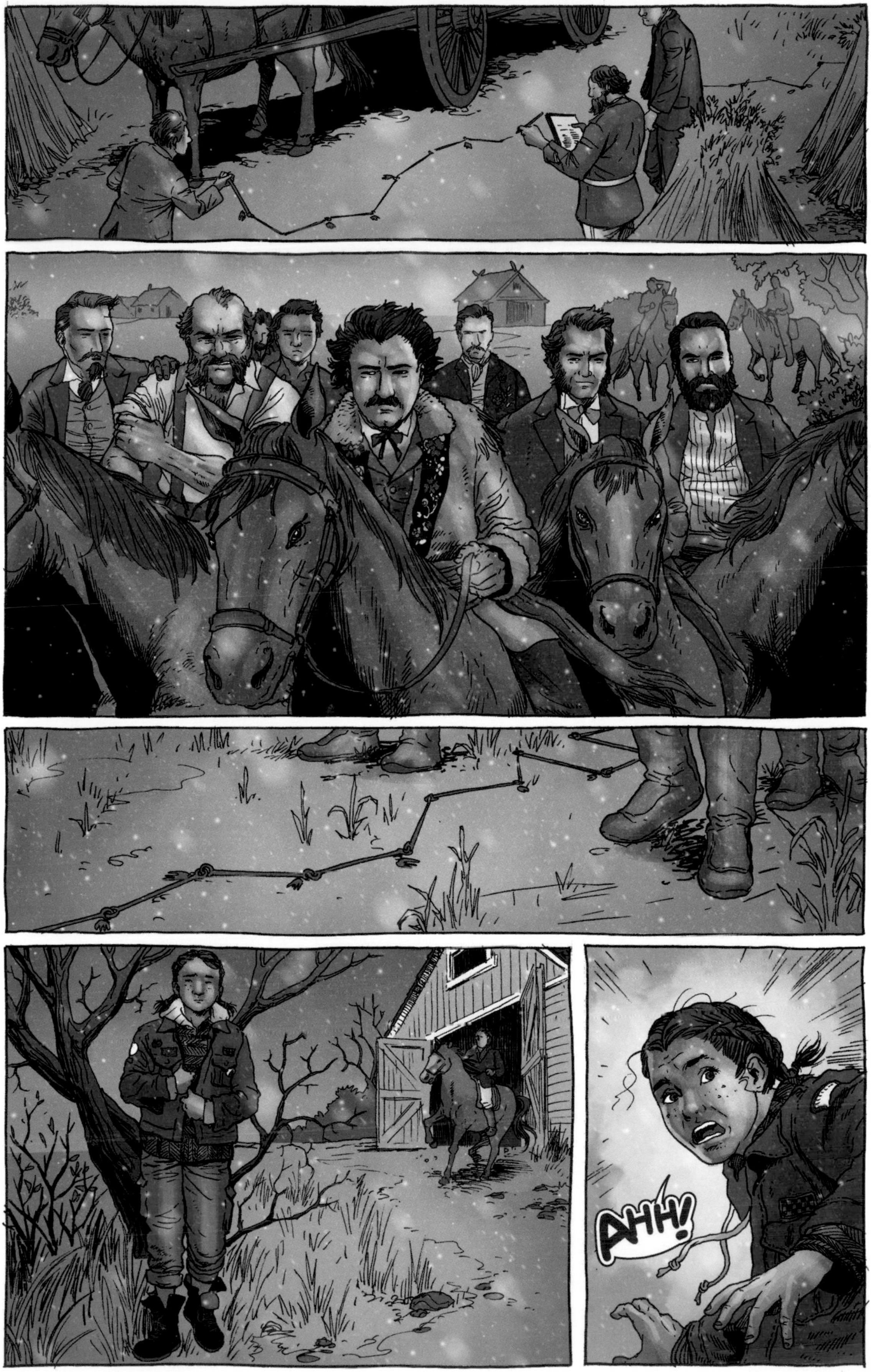
AHH!

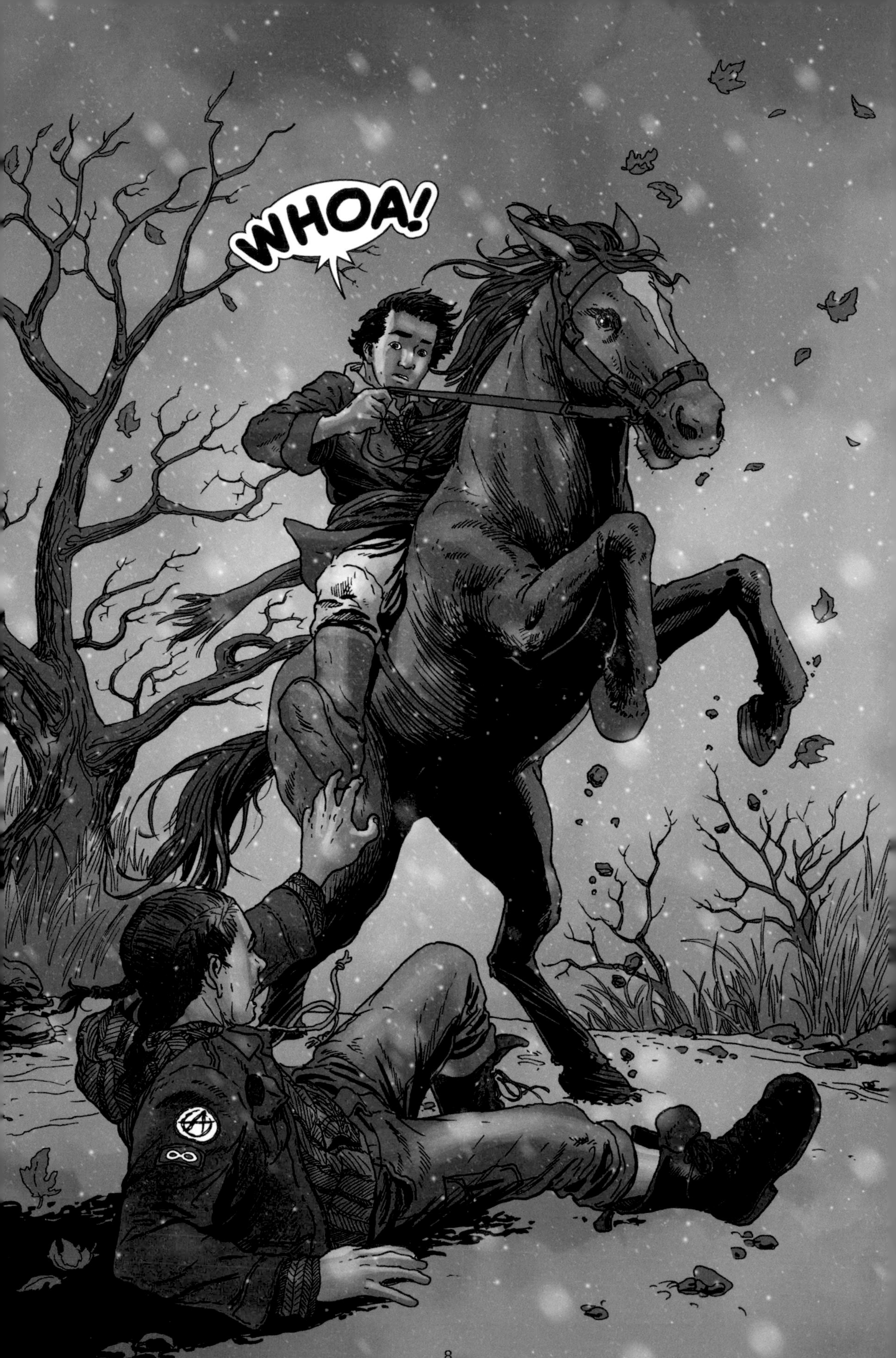
WHOA!

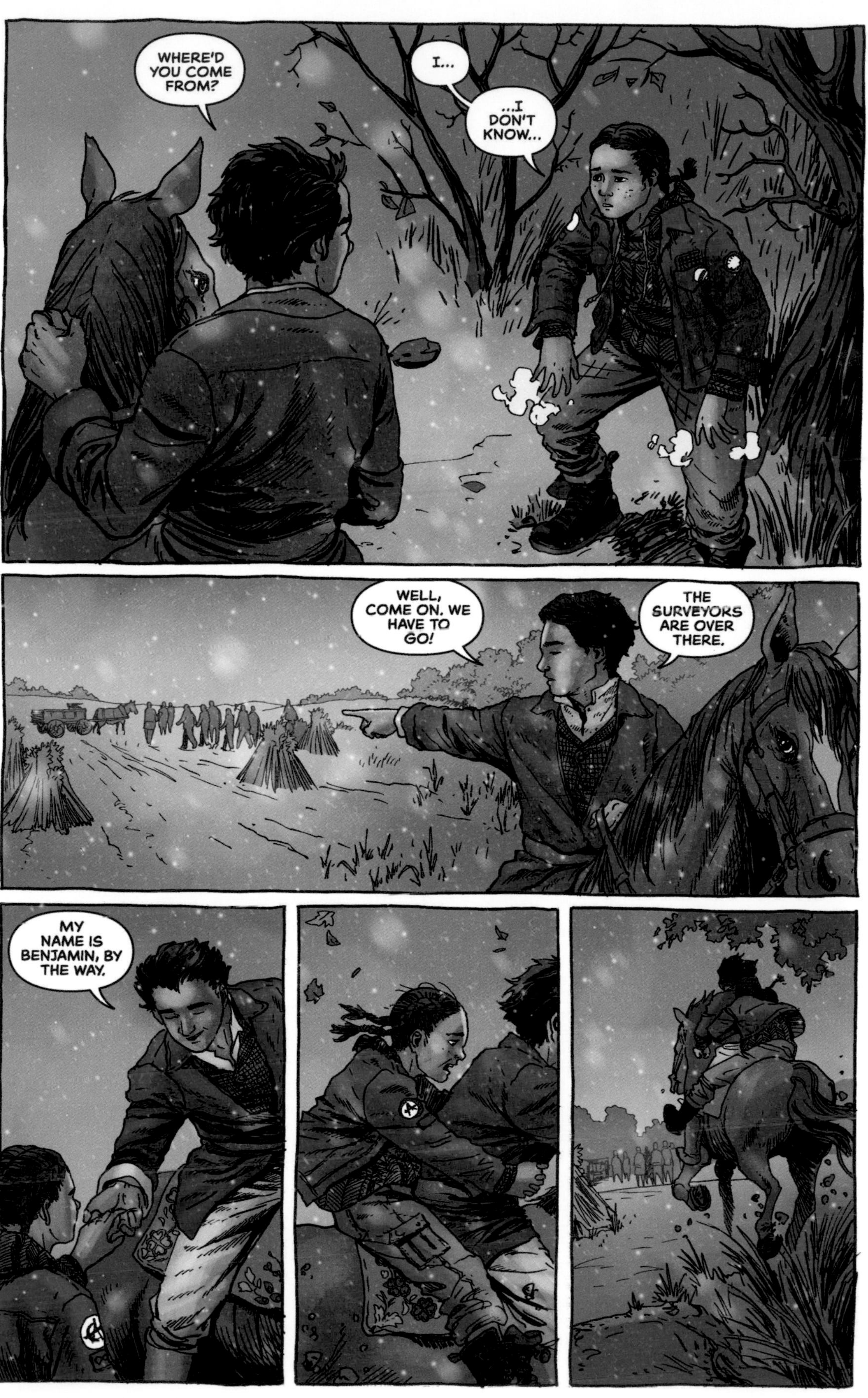
WHERE'D YOU COME FROM?
I...
...I DON'T KNOW...
WELL, COME ON. WE HAVE TO GO!
THE SURVEYORS ARE OVER THERE.
MY NAME IS BENJAMIN, BY THE WAY.

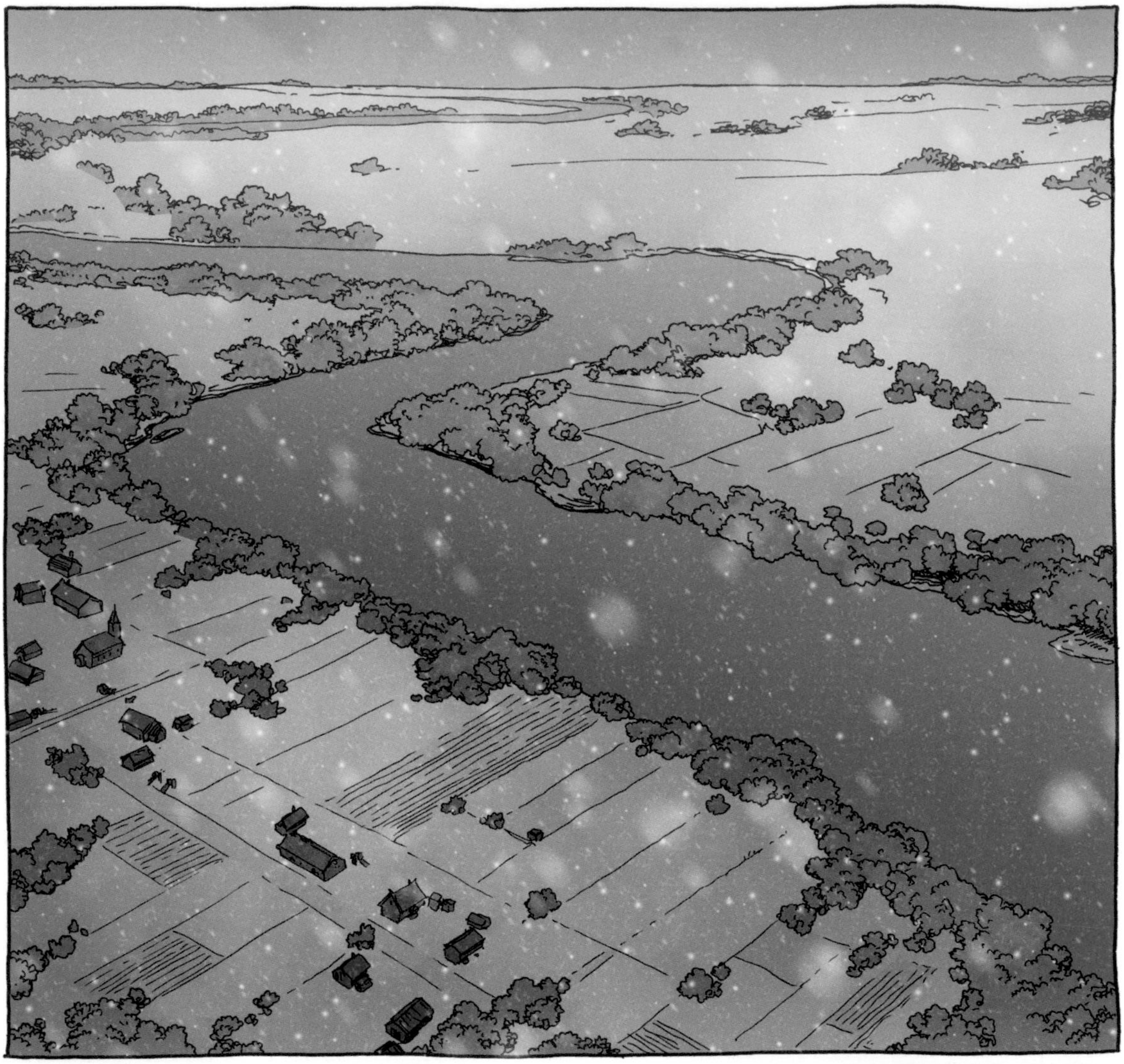

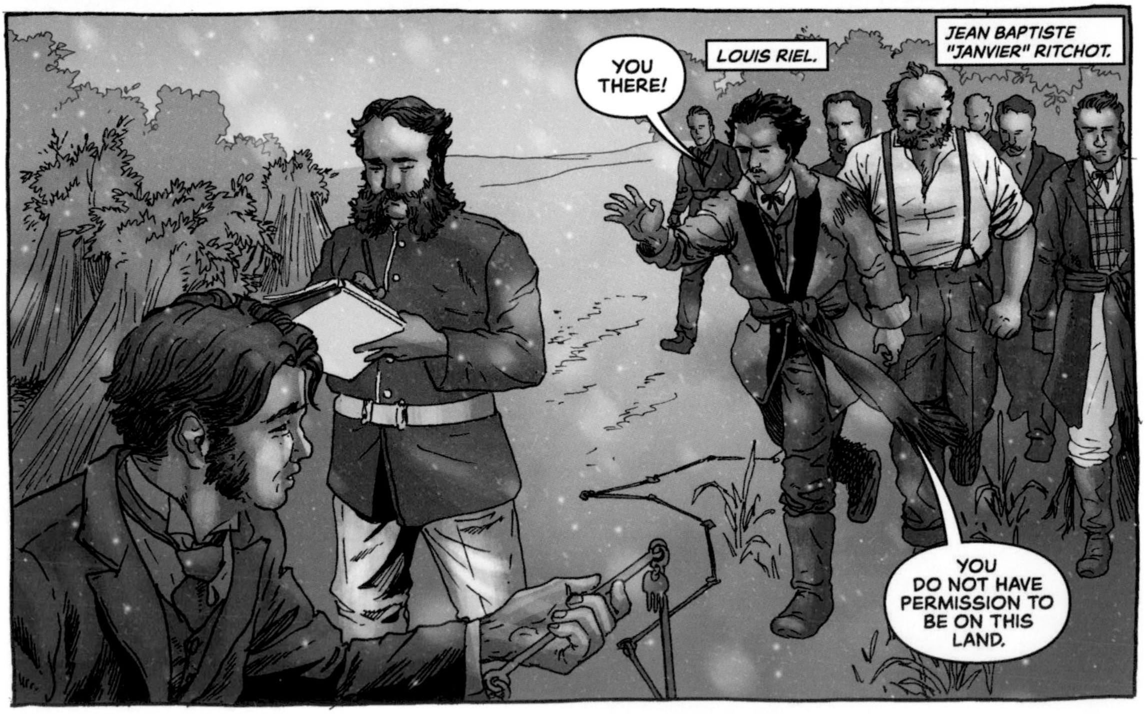
LOUIS RIEL.
JEAN BAPTISTE "JANVIER" RITCHOT.
YOU THERE!
YOU DO NOT HAVE PERMISSION TO BE ON THIS LAND.

I AM MAJOR WEBB.
I AM SURVEYING THIS LAND ON BEHALF OF THE CROWN AND DOMINION OF CANADA.
THIS IS NOT A PART OF CANADA YET, SIR.
THIS IS *MÉTIS LAND.*
NO ONE HAS GIVEN YOU PERMISSION TO DO THIS.
WE ARE TASKED WITH SURVEYING THE ENTIRE AREA OF RED RIVER.
YOU CANNOT STOP US.
WE ARE HERE UNDER THE AUTHORITY OF--
*ARRÊTE AVANT DE TE FAIRE ARRÊTER!**
**STOP BEFORE I MAKE YOU STOP!*

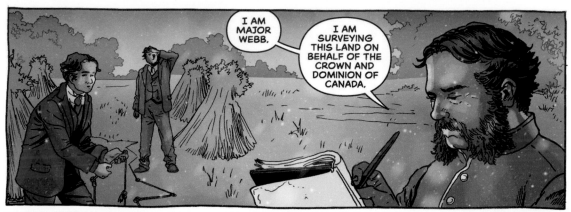

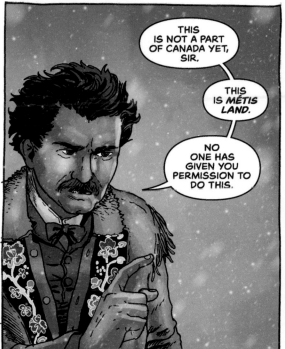

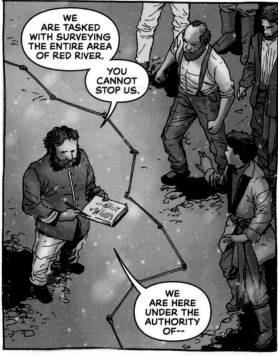

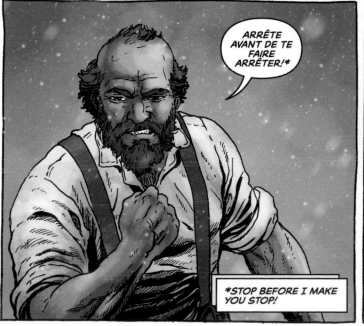

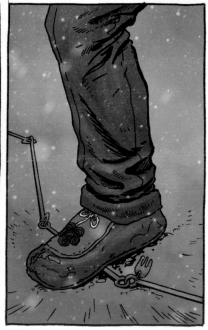

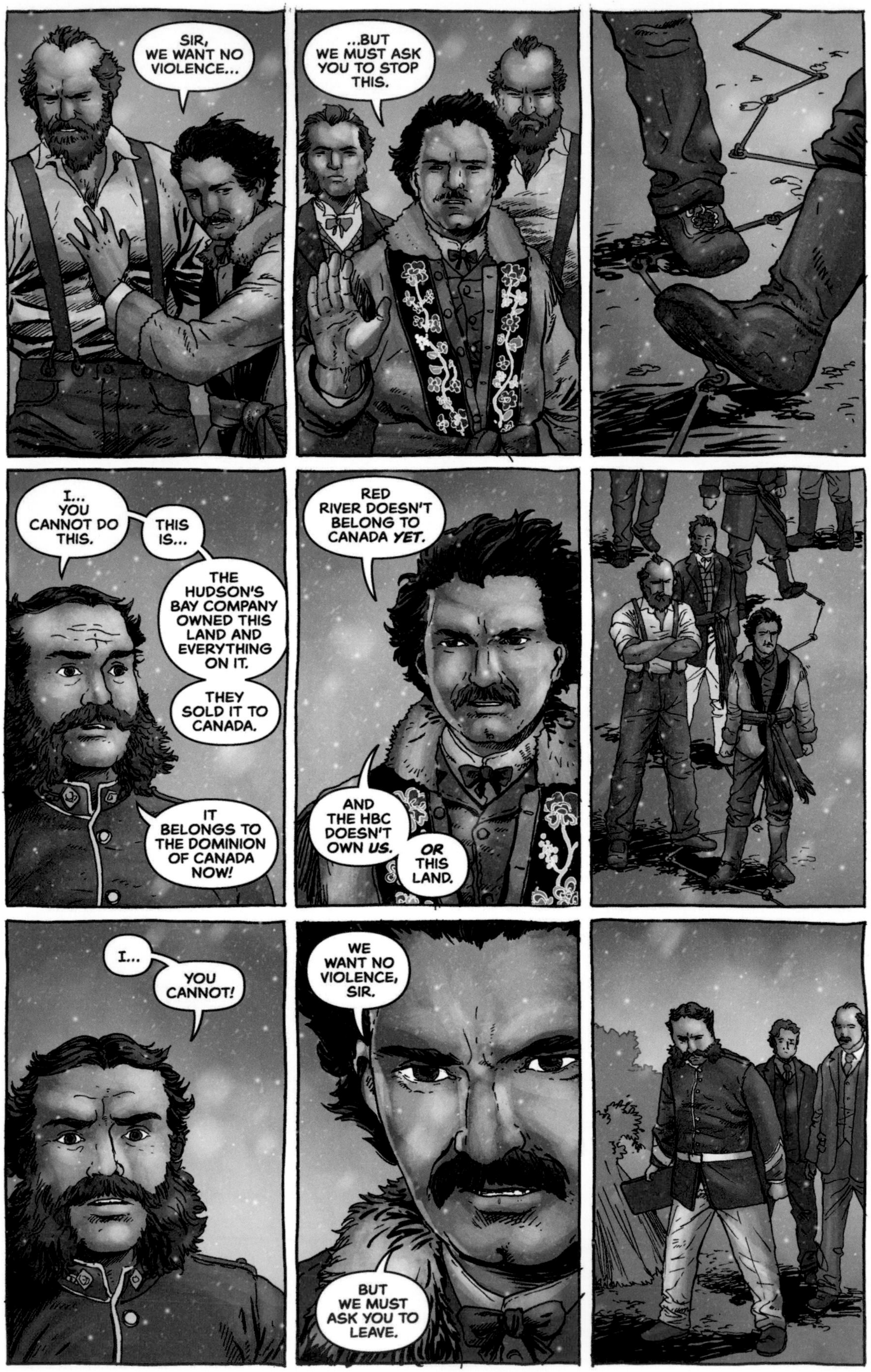
SIR, WE WANT NO VIOLENCE...
...BUT WE MUST ASK YOU TO STOP THIS.
I... YOU CANNOT DO THIS.
THIS IS...
THE HUDSON'S BAY COMPANY OWNED THIS LAND AND EVERYTHING ON IT.
THEY SOLD IT TO CANADA.
IT BELONGS TO THE DOMINION OF CANADA NOW!
RED RIVER DOESN'T BELONG TO CANADA *YET*.
AND THE HBC DOESN'T OWN *US*.
OR THIS LAND.
I...
YOU CANNOT!
WE WANT NO VIOLENCE, SIR.
BUT WE MUST ASK YOU TO LEAVE.

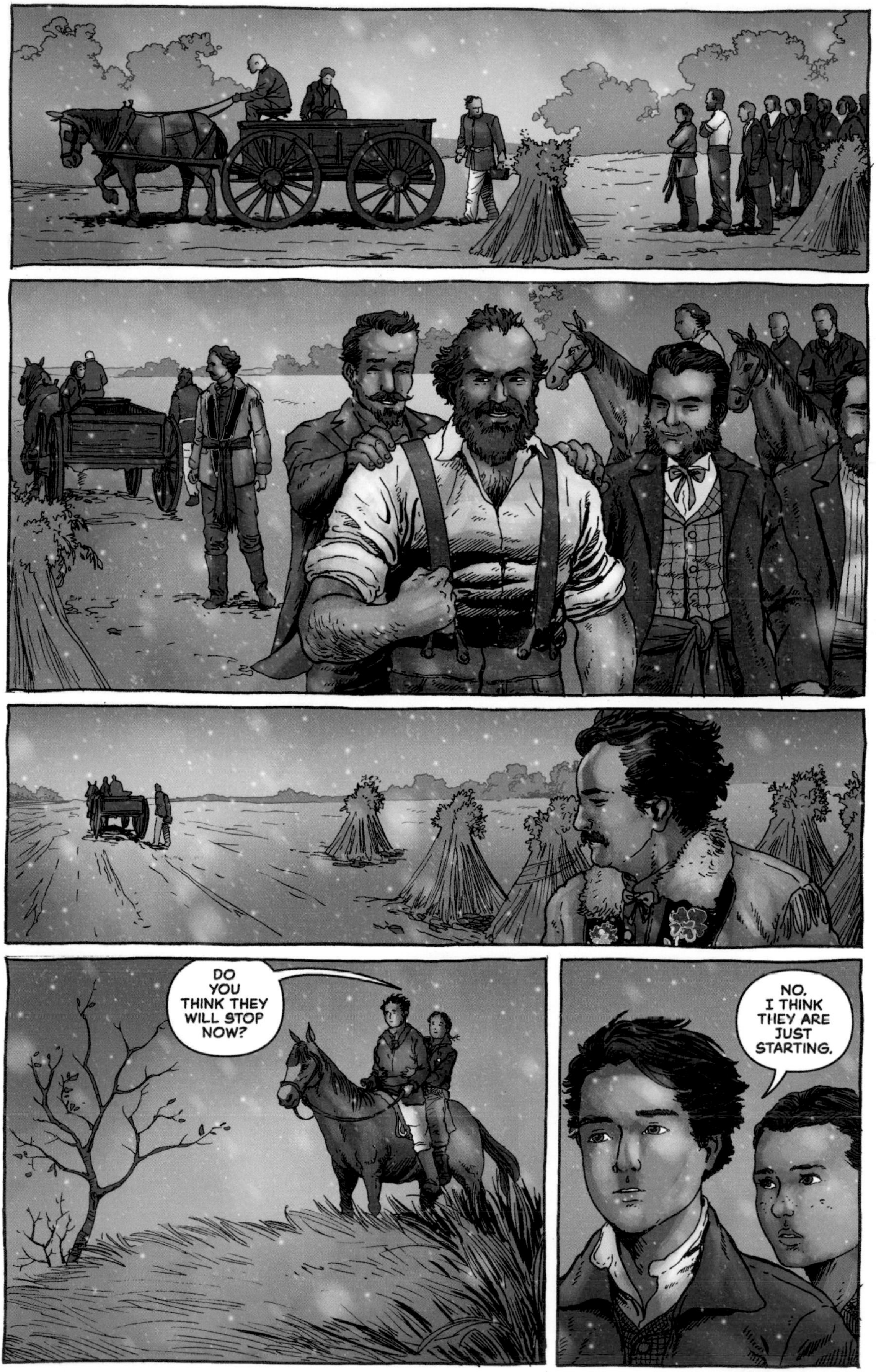
DO YOU THINK THEY WILL STOP NOW?
NO. I THINK THEY ARE JUST STARTING.

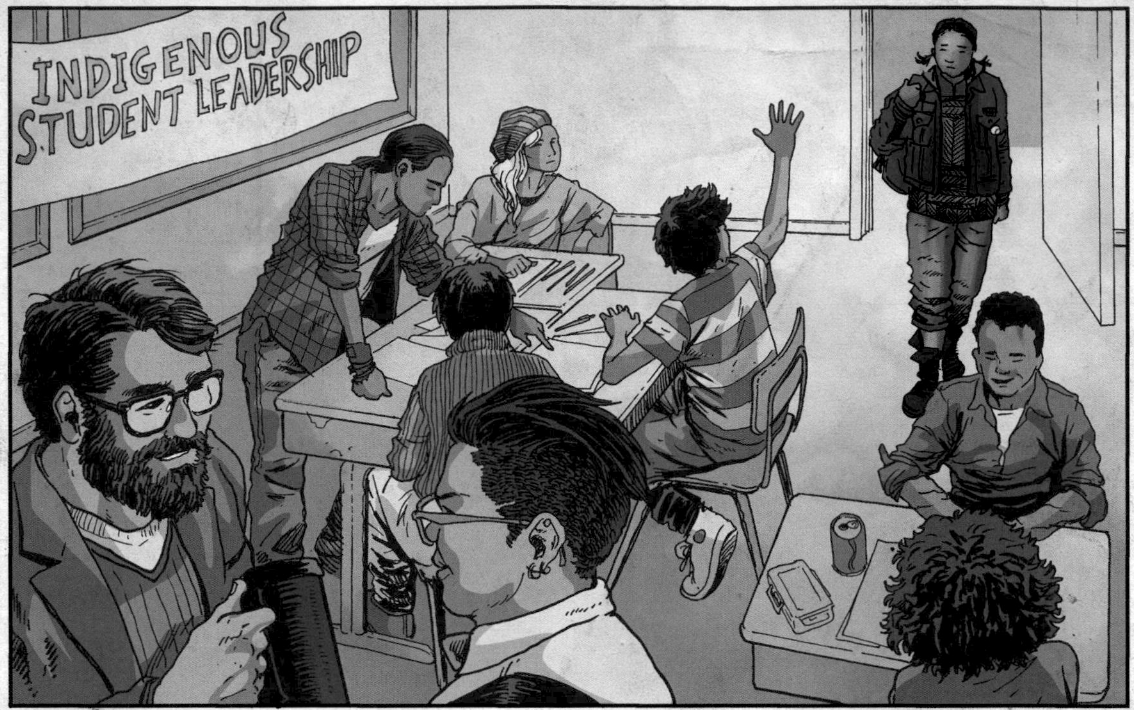
INDIGENOUS STUDENT LEADERSHIP

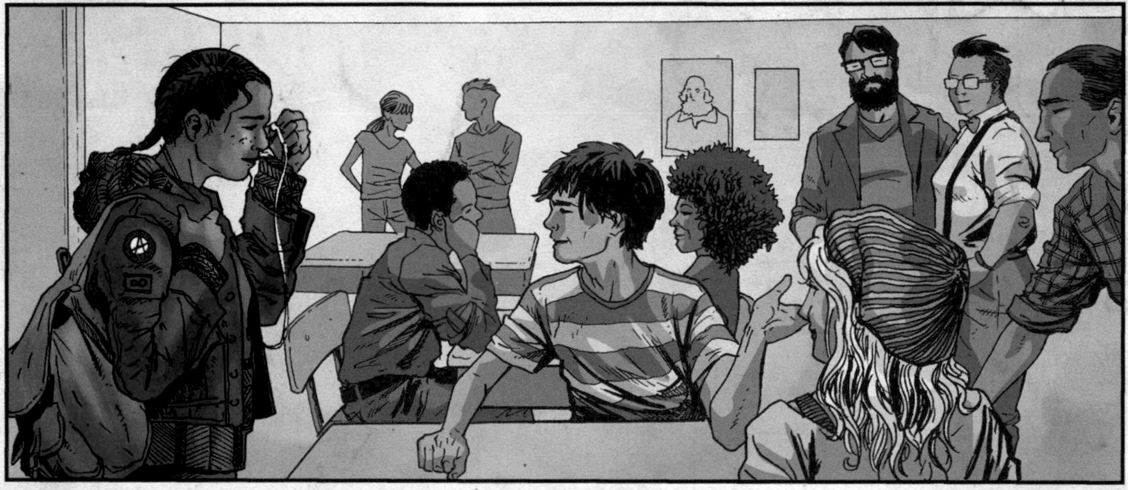

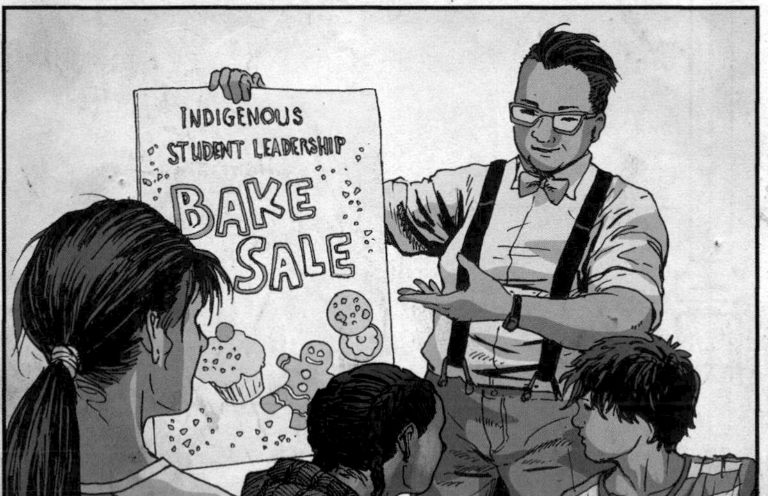
INDIGENOUS
STUDENT LEADERSHIP
BAKE SALE

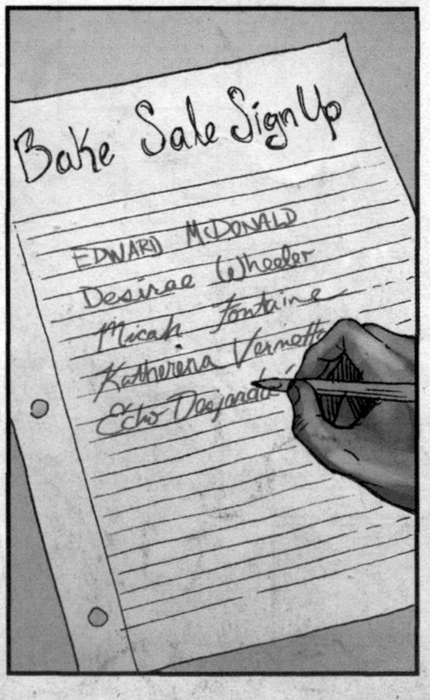
Bake Sale Sign Up
EDWARD McDONALD
Desirae Wheeler
Micah Fontaine
Katherena Vernett
Echo Desjard

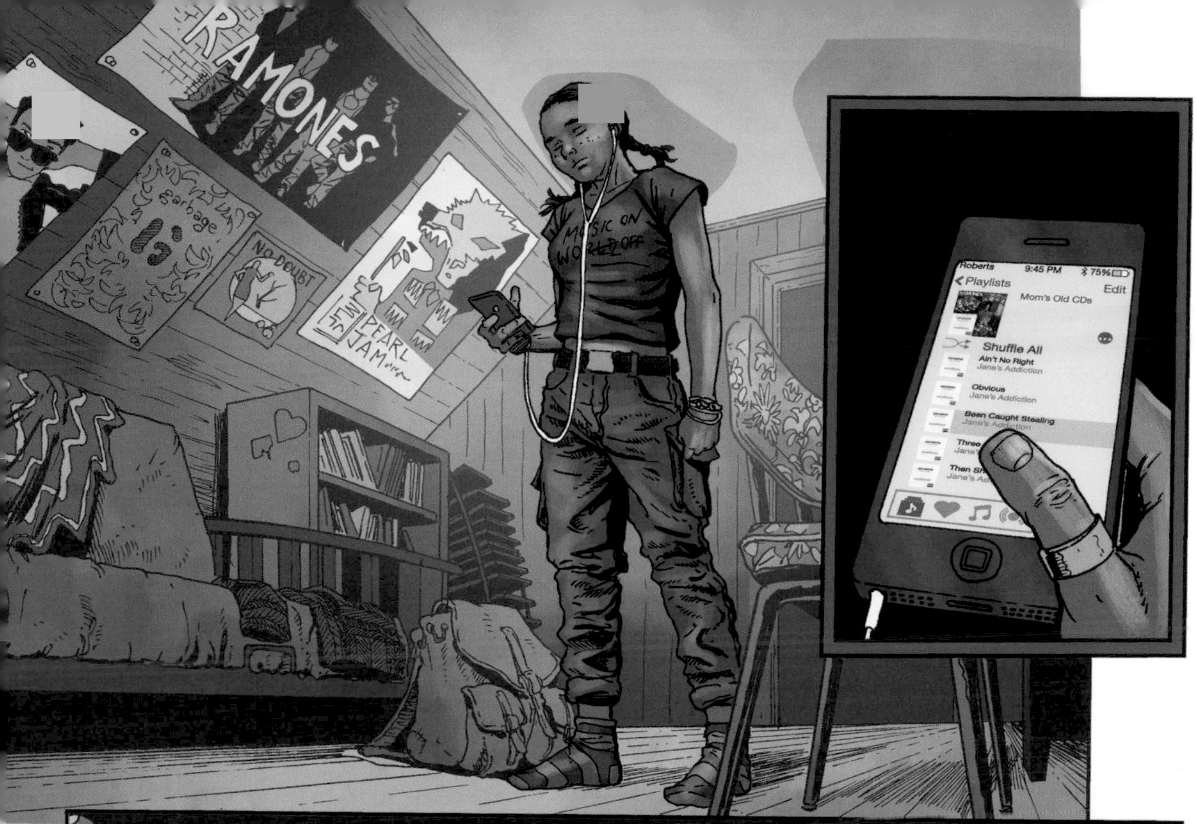
RAMONES
garbage
NO DOUBT
PEARL JAM
MUSIC ON WORLD OFF
Roberts
9:45 PM
75%
Playlists
Edit
Mom's Old CDs
Shuffle All
Ain't No Right
Jane's Addiction
Obvious
Jane's Addiction
Been Caught Stealing
Jane's Addiction

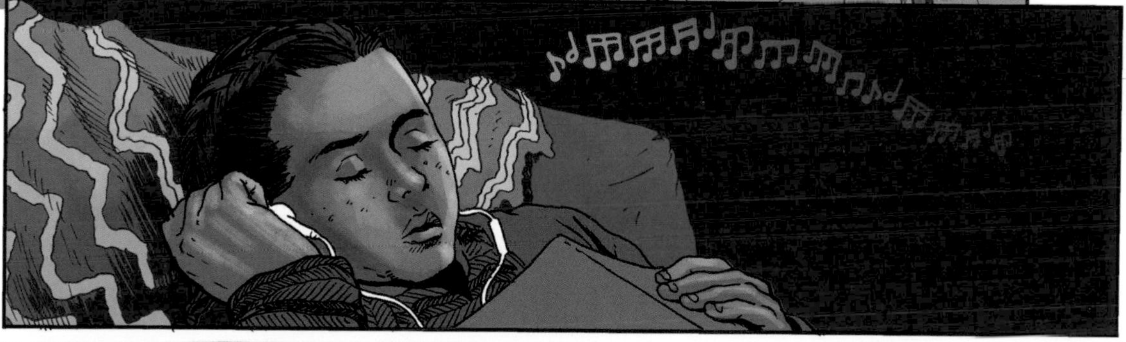

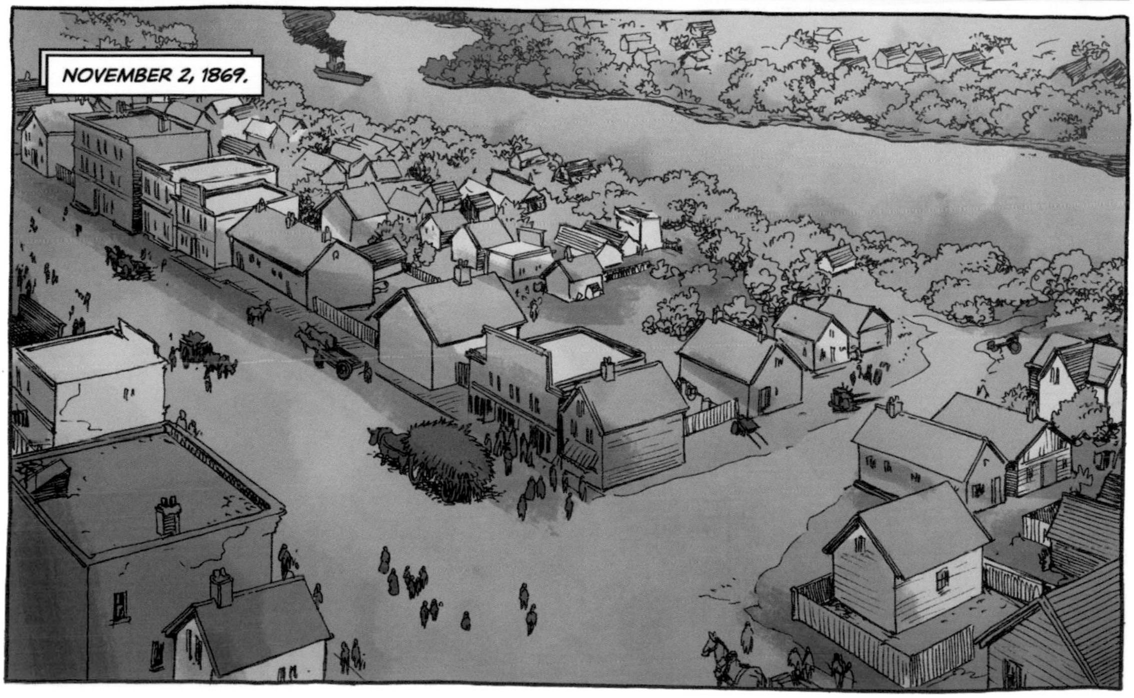
NOVEMBER 2, 1869.

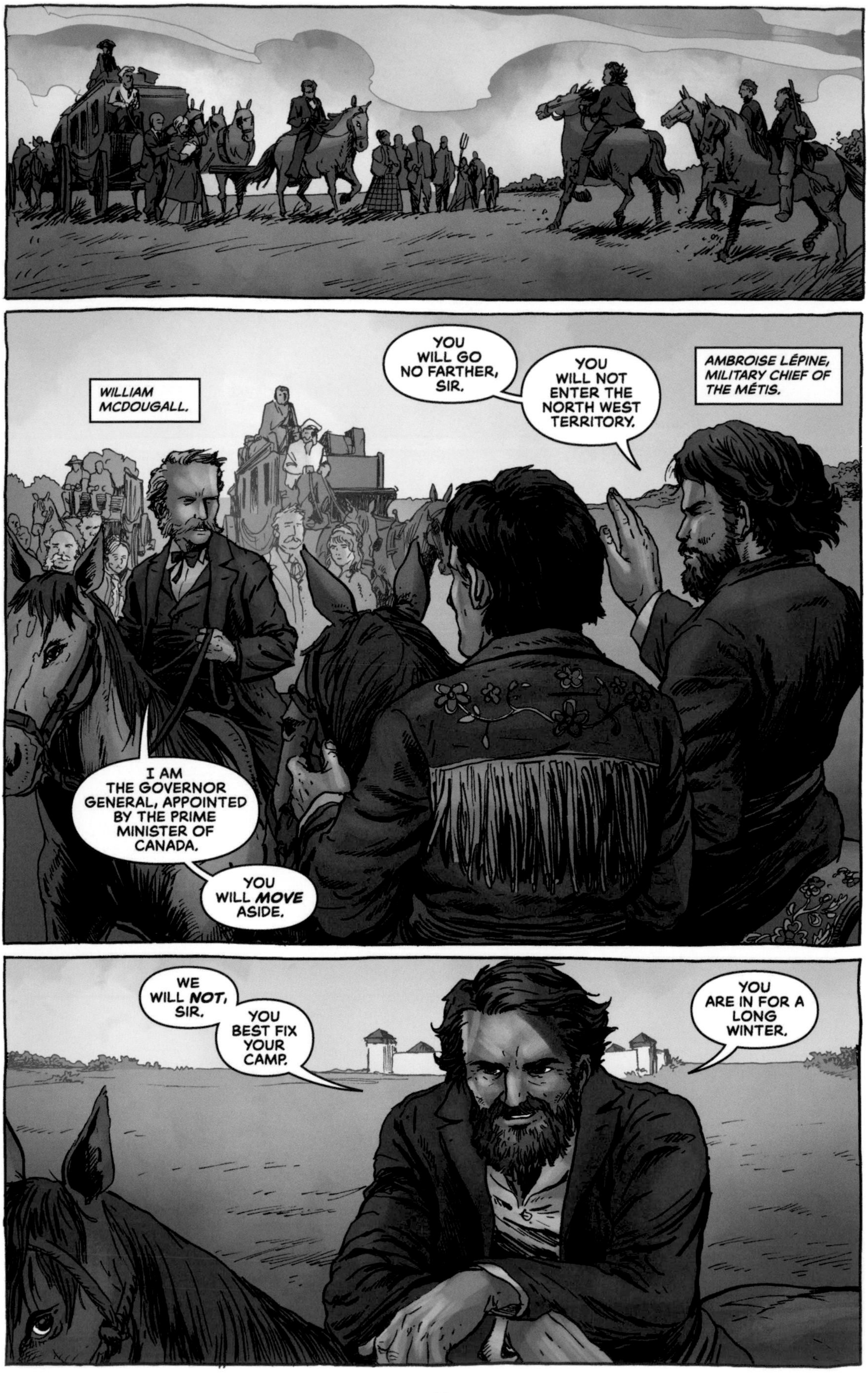
WILLIAM MCDOUGALL.
YOU WILL GO NO FARTHER, SIR.
YOU WILL NOT ENTER THE NORTH WEST TERRITORY.
AMBROISE LÉPINE, MILITARY CHIEF OF THE MÉTIS.
I AM THE GOVERNOR GENERAL, APPOINTED BY THE PRIME MINISTER OF CANADA.
YOU WILL MOVE ASIDE.
WE WILL NOT, SIR.
YOU BEST FIX YOUR CAMP.
YOU ARE IN FOR A LONG WINTER.

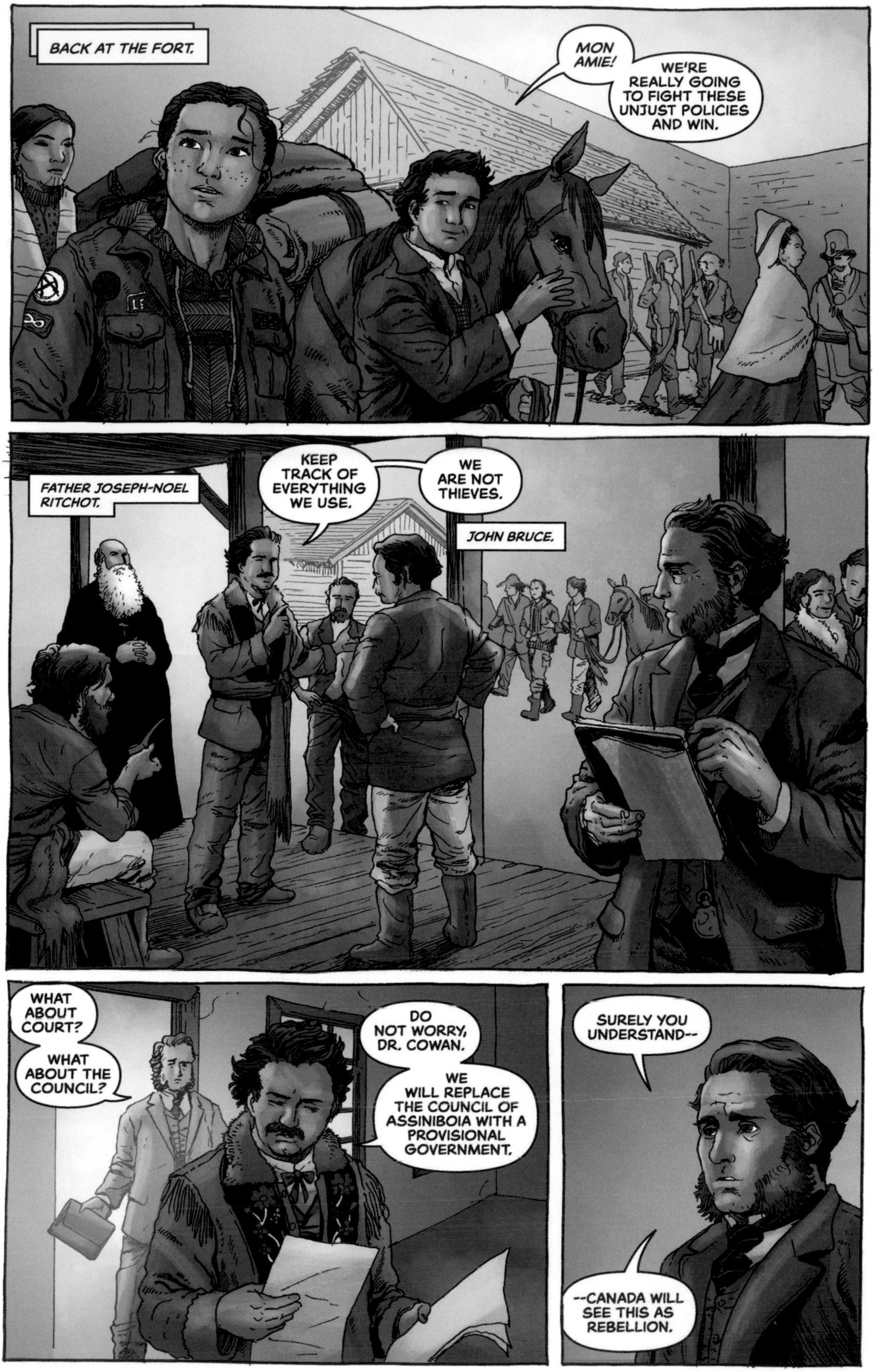
BACK AT THE FORT.
MON AMIE!
WE'RE REALLY GOING TO FIGHT THESE UNJUST POLICIES AND WIN.
FATHER JOSEPH-NOEL RITCHOT.
KEEP TRACK OF EVERYTHING WE USE.
WE ARE NOT THIEVES.
JOHN BRUCE.
WHAT ABOUT COURT?
WHAT ABOUT THE COUNCIL?
DO NOT WORRY, DR. COWAN.
WE WILL REPLACE THE COUNCIL OF ASSINIBOIA WITH A PROVISIONAL GOVERNMENT.
SURELY YOU UNDERSTAND--
--CANADA WILL SEE THIS AS REBELLION.

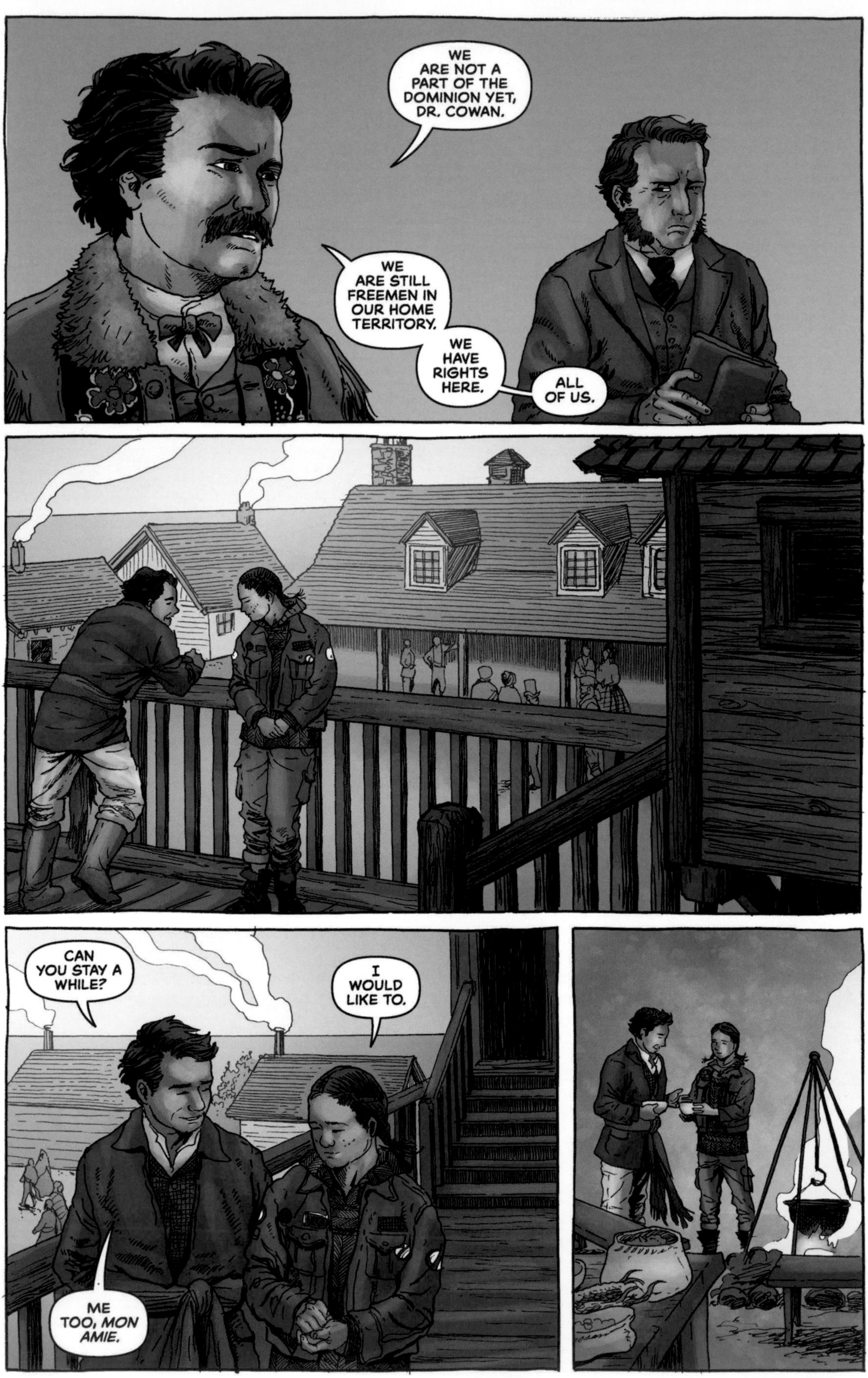
WE ARE NOT A PART OF THE DOMINION YET, DR. COWAN.
WE ARE STILL FREEMEN IN OUR HOME TERRITORY.
WE HAVE RIGHTS HERE.
ALL OF US.
CAN YOU STAY A WHILE?
I WOULD LIKE TO.
ME TOO, MON AMIE.

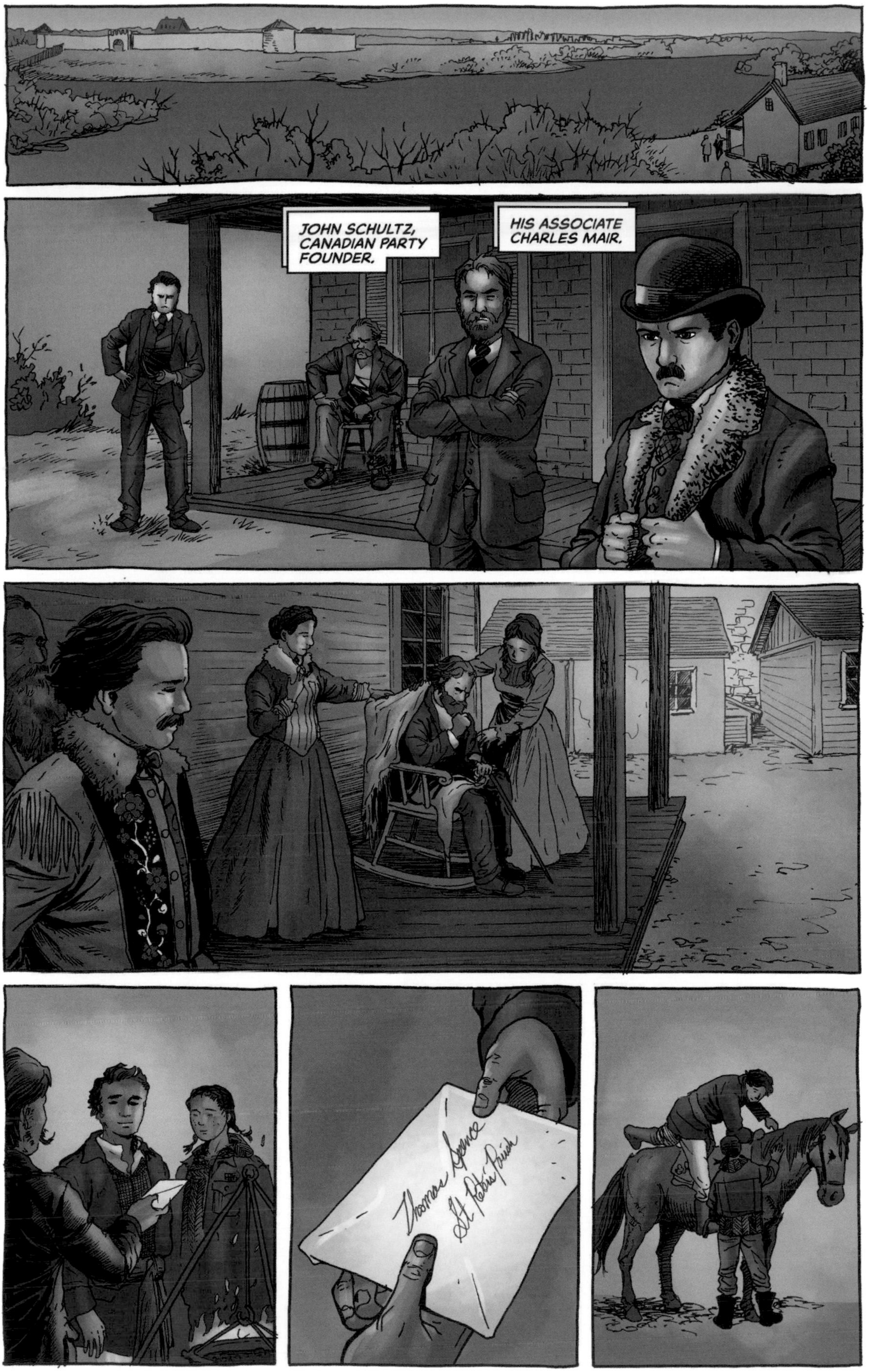
JOHN SCHULTZ, CANADIAN PARTY FOUNDER.
HIS ASSOCIATE CHARLES MAIR.
Thomas Spence
St Peter's Parish

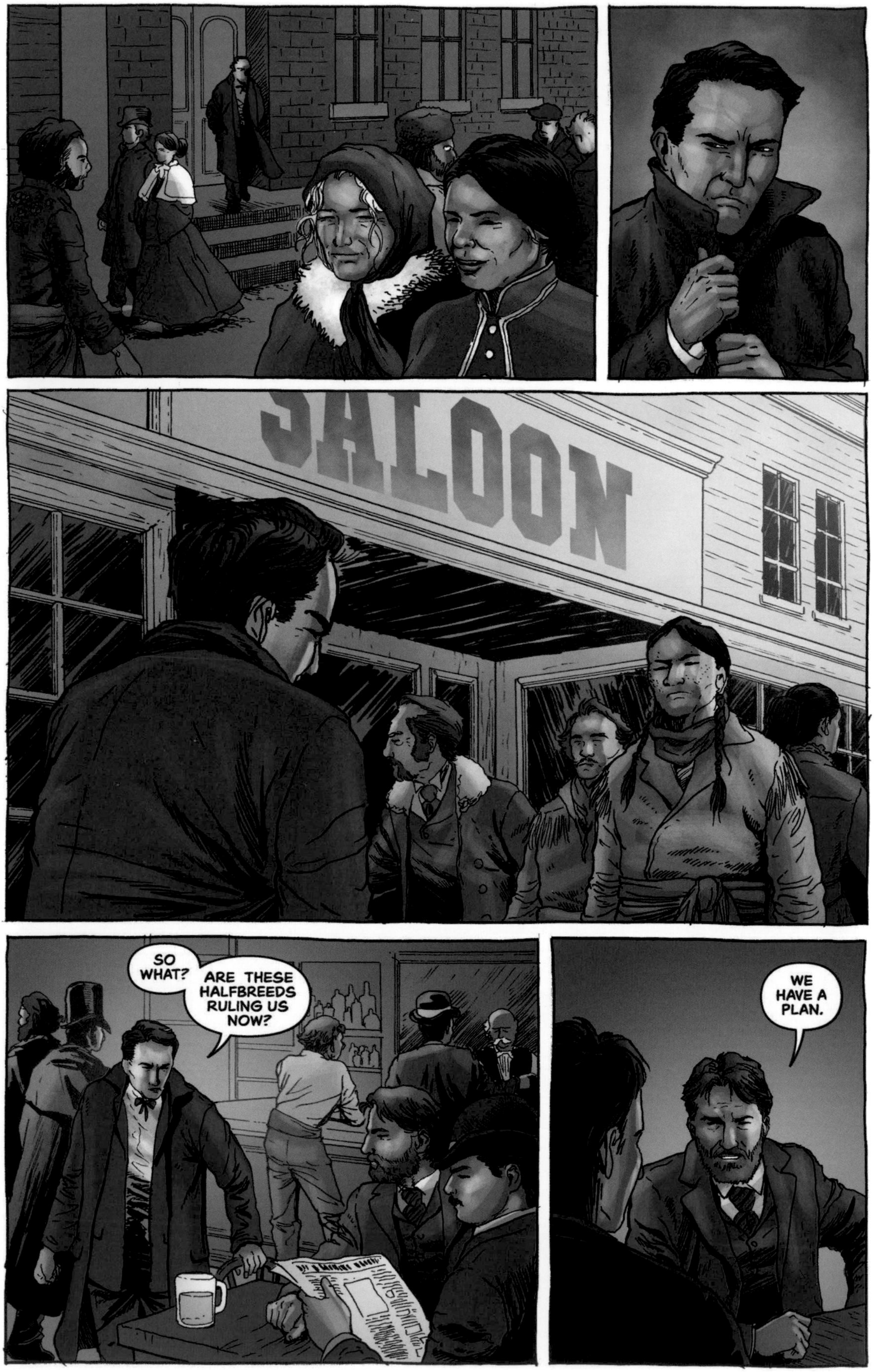
SALOON
SO WHAT?
ARE THESE HALFBREEDS RULING US NOW?
WE HAVE A PLAN.

WE SHOULD IMPRISON THEM AND KEEP THEM OUT OF TROUBLE.

WE CAN DO SO WITHOUT BLOODSHED.

WE SHOULD GO OUT AND MEET THEM THEN.

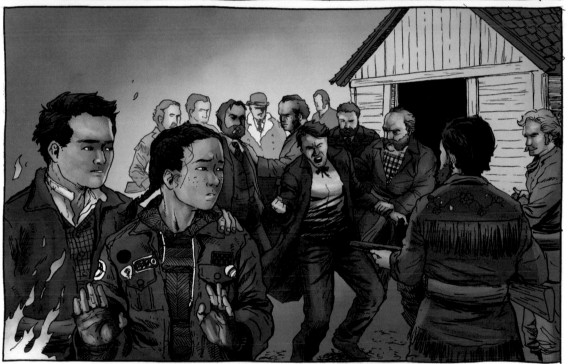

25

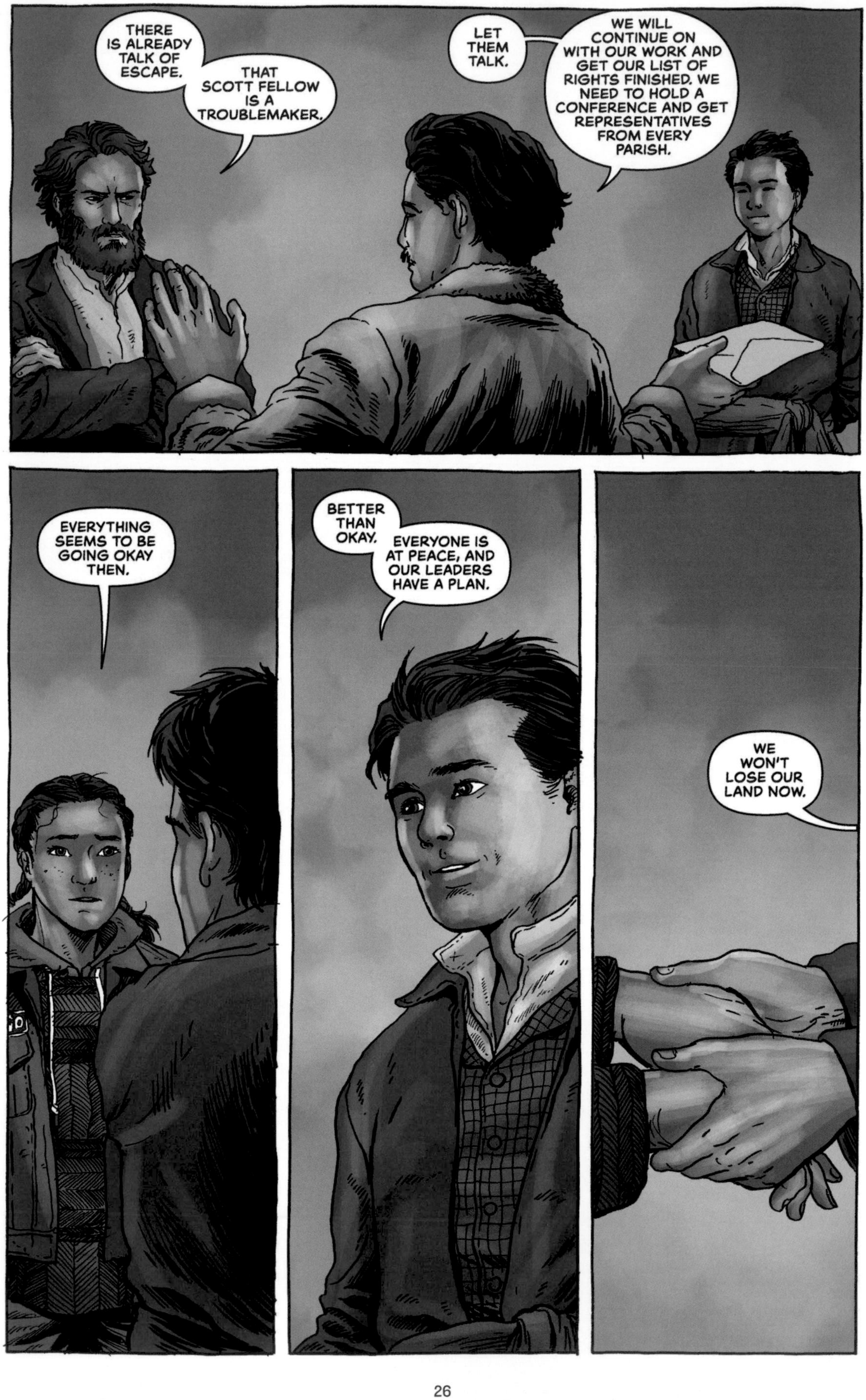
THERE IS ALREADY TALK OF ESCAPE.
THAT SCOTT FELLOW IS A TROUBLEMAKER.
LET THEM TALK.
WE WILL CONTINUE ON WITH OUR WORK AND GET OUR LIST OF RIGHTS FINISHED. WE NEED TO HOLD A CONFERENCE AND GET REPRESENTATIVES FROM EVERY PARISH.
EVERYTHING SEEMS TO BE GOING OKAY THEN.
BETTER THAN OKAY.
EVERYONE IS AT PEACE, AND OUR LEADERS HAVE A PLAN.
WE WON'T LOSE OUR LAND NOW.

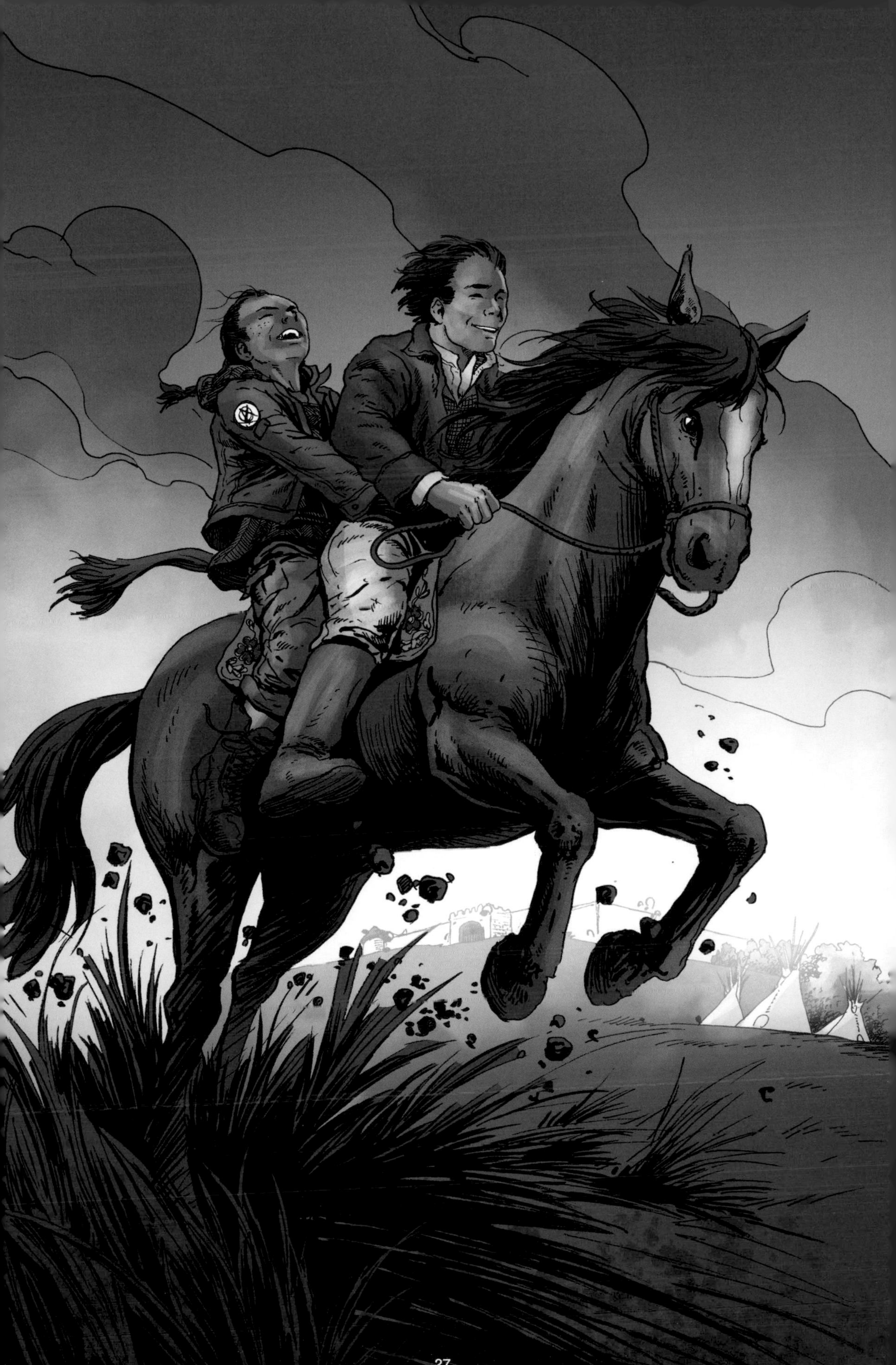

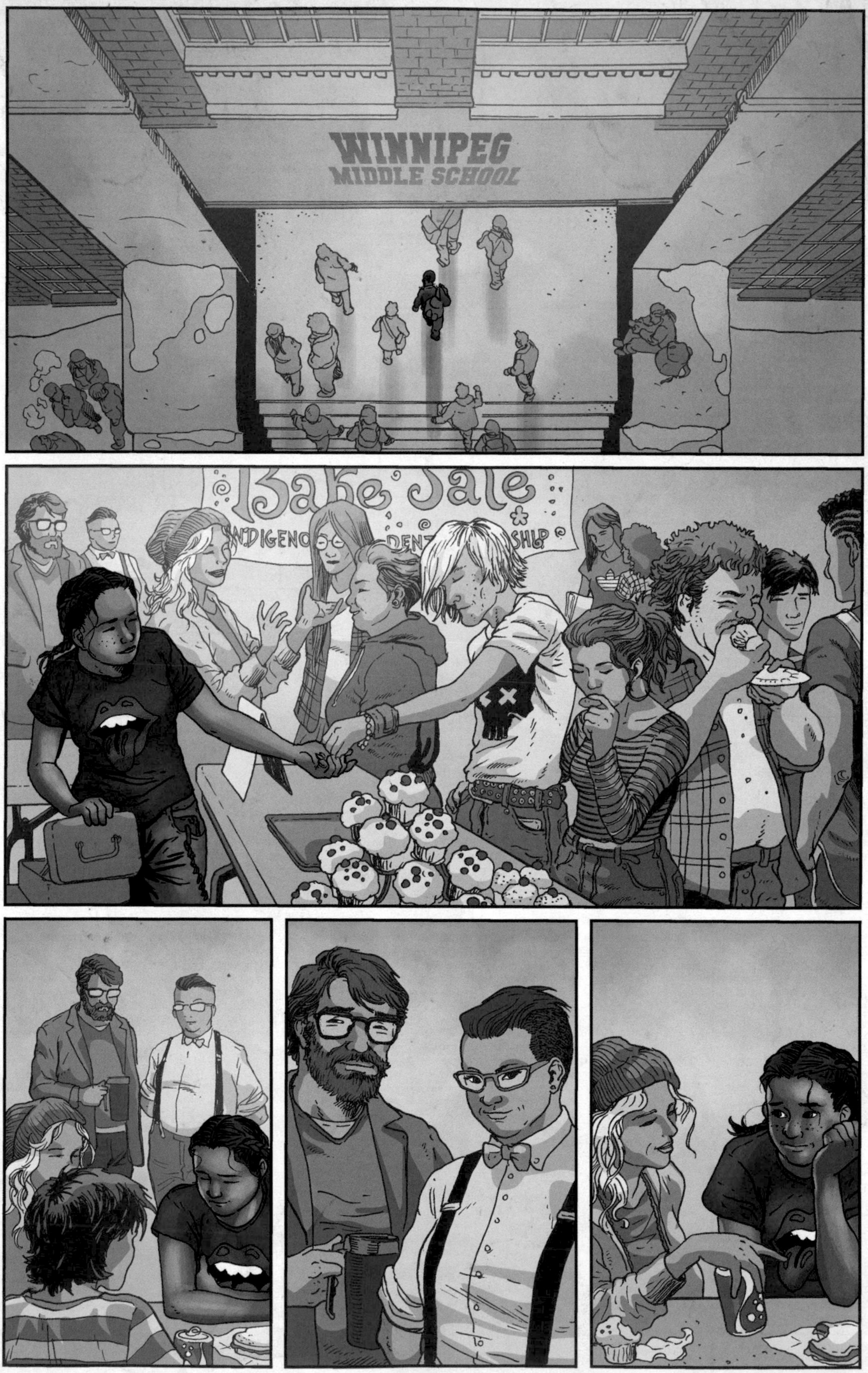
WINNIPEG
MIDDLE SCHOOL
Bake Sale

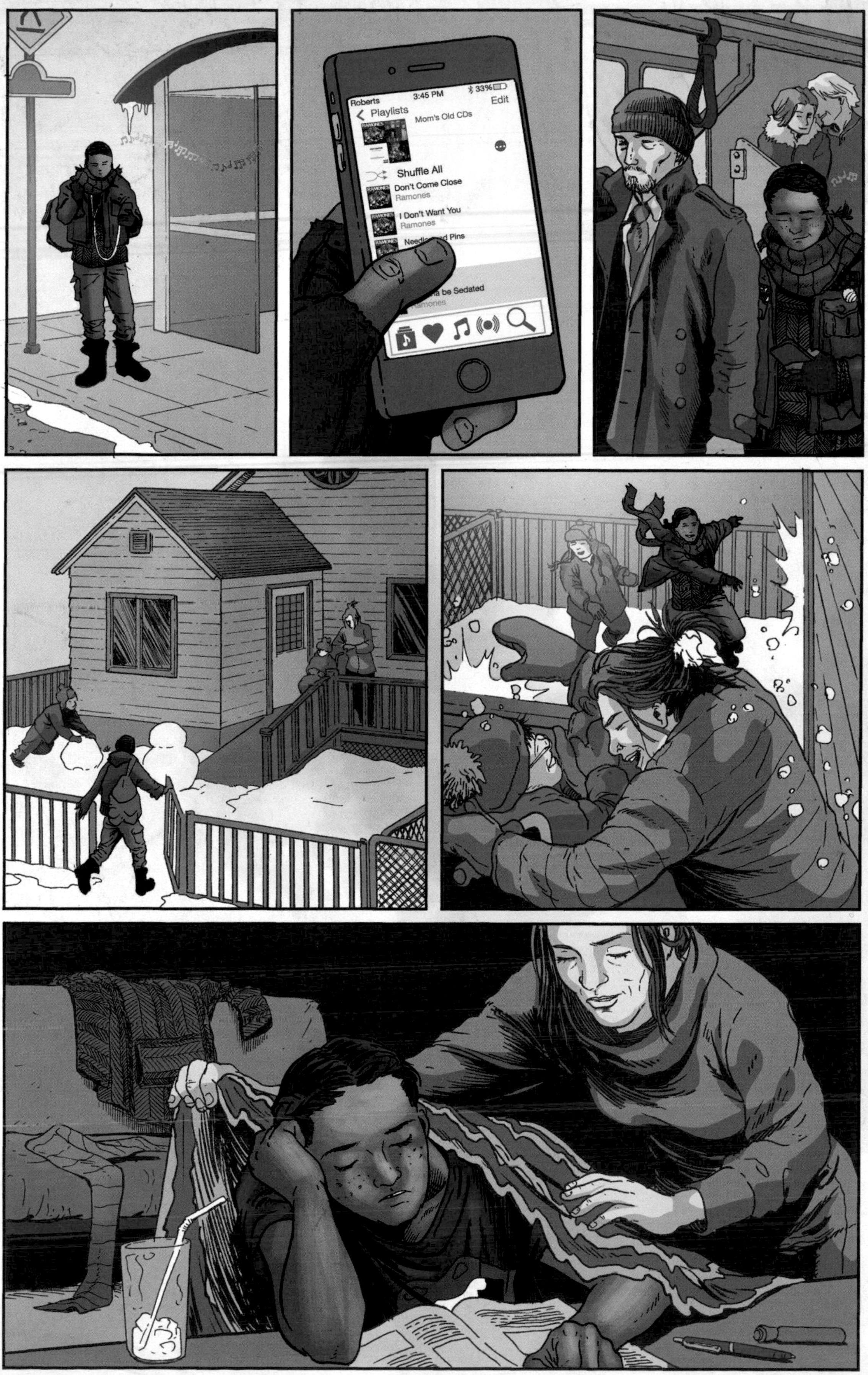
Roberts
3:45 PM
33%
Edit
Playlists
Mom's Old CDs
Shuffle All
Don't Come Close
Ramones
I Don't Want You
Ramones

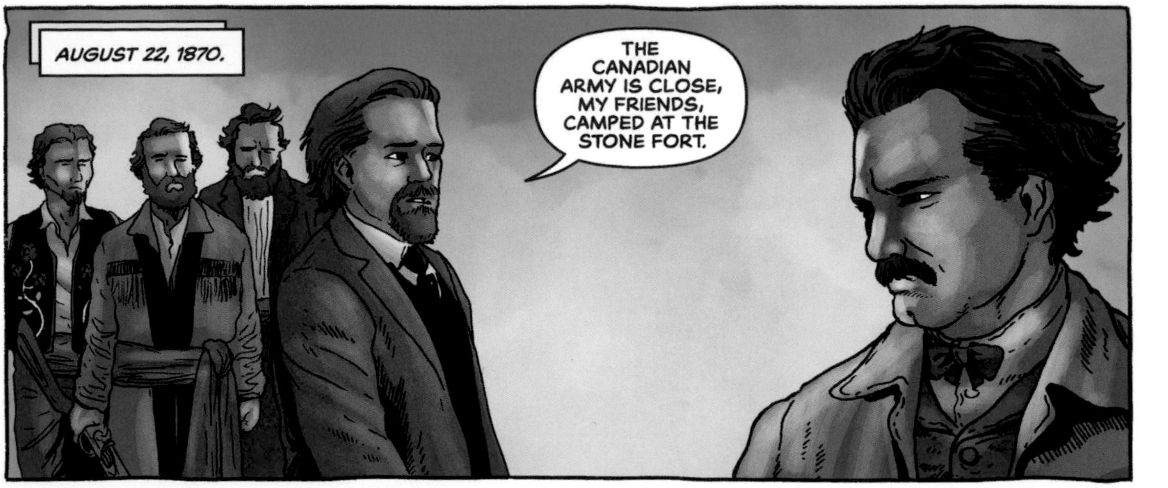
AUGUST 22, 1870.
THE CANADIAN ARMY IS CLOSE, MY FRIENDS, CAMPED AT THE STONE FORT.

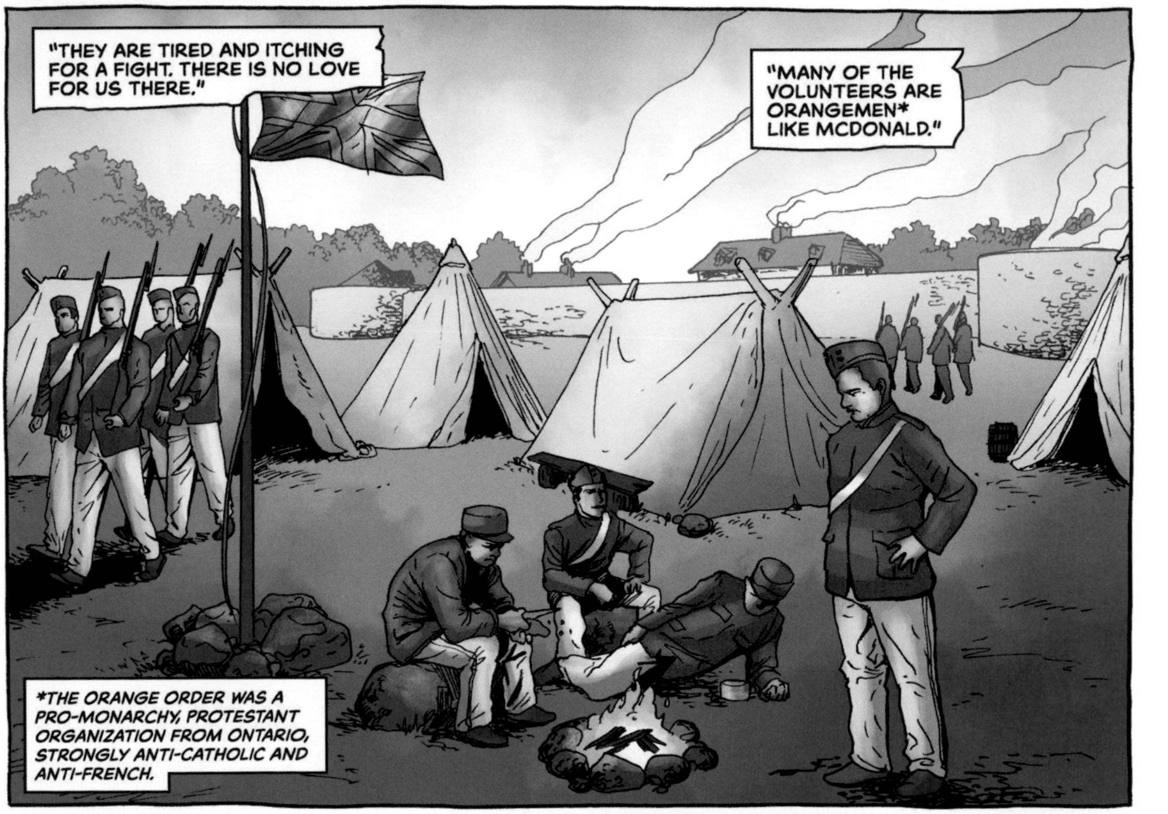
"THEY ARE TIRED AND ITCHING FOR A FIGHT. THERE IS NO LOVE FOR US THERE."
"MANY OF THE VOLUNTEERS ARE ORANGEMEN* LIKE MCDONALD."
*THE ORANGE ORDER WAS A PRO-MONARCHY, PROTESTANT ORGANIZATION FROM ONTARIO, STRONGLY ANTI-CATHOLIC AND ANTI-FRENCH.

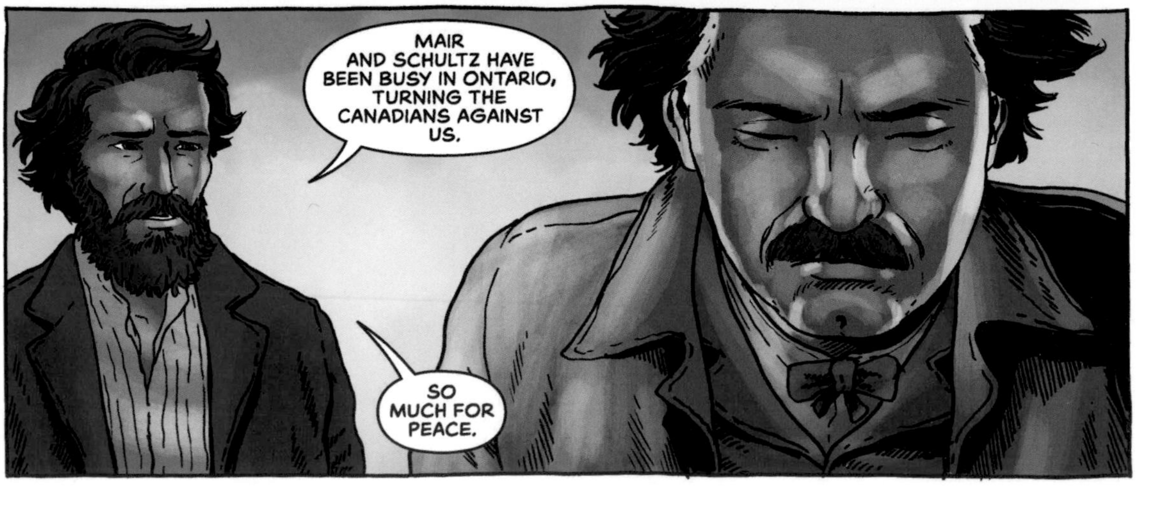
MAIR AND SCHULTZ HAVE BEEN BUSY IN ONTARIO, TURNING THE CANADIANS AGAINST US.
SO MUCH FOR PEACE.

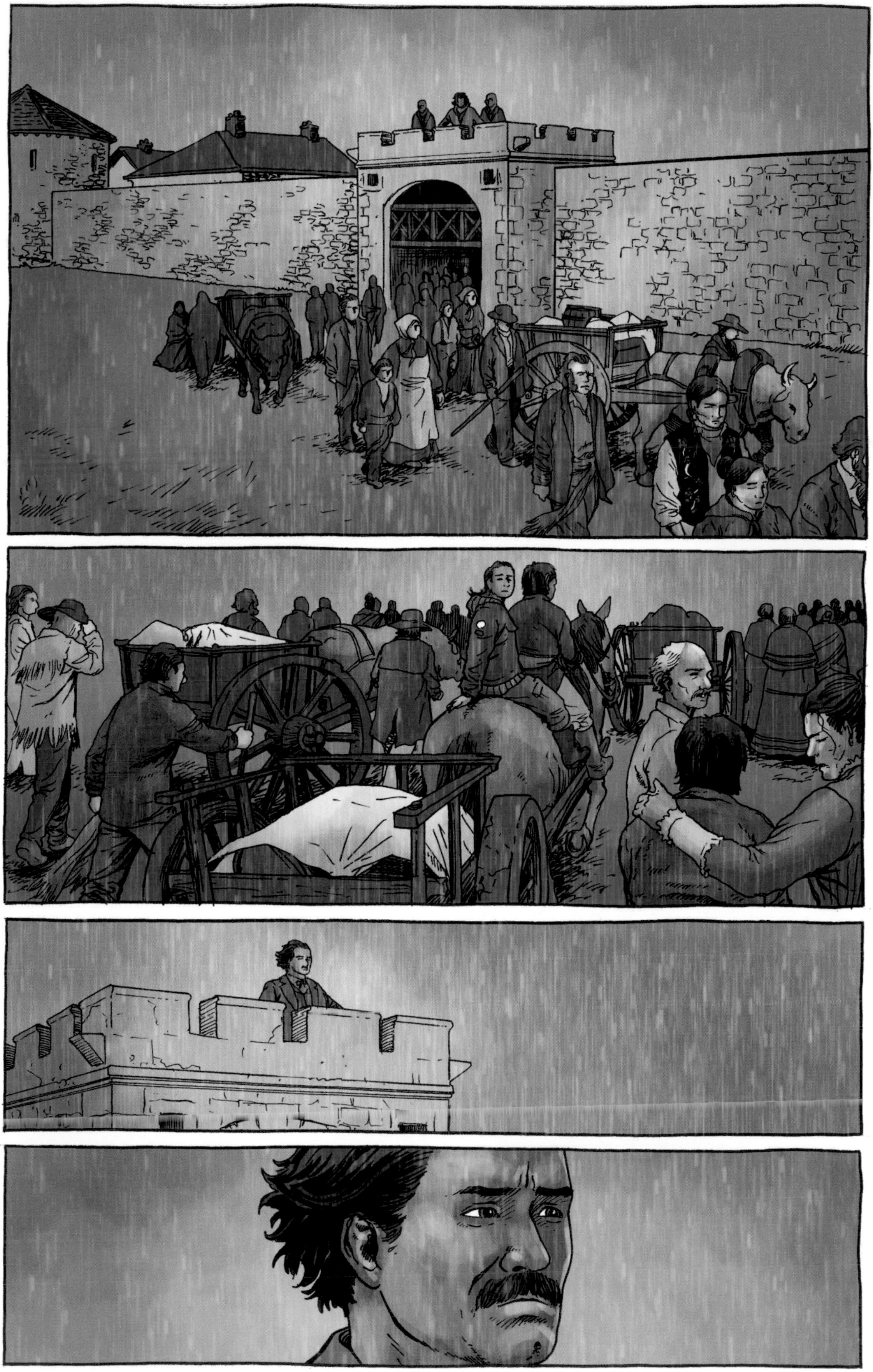

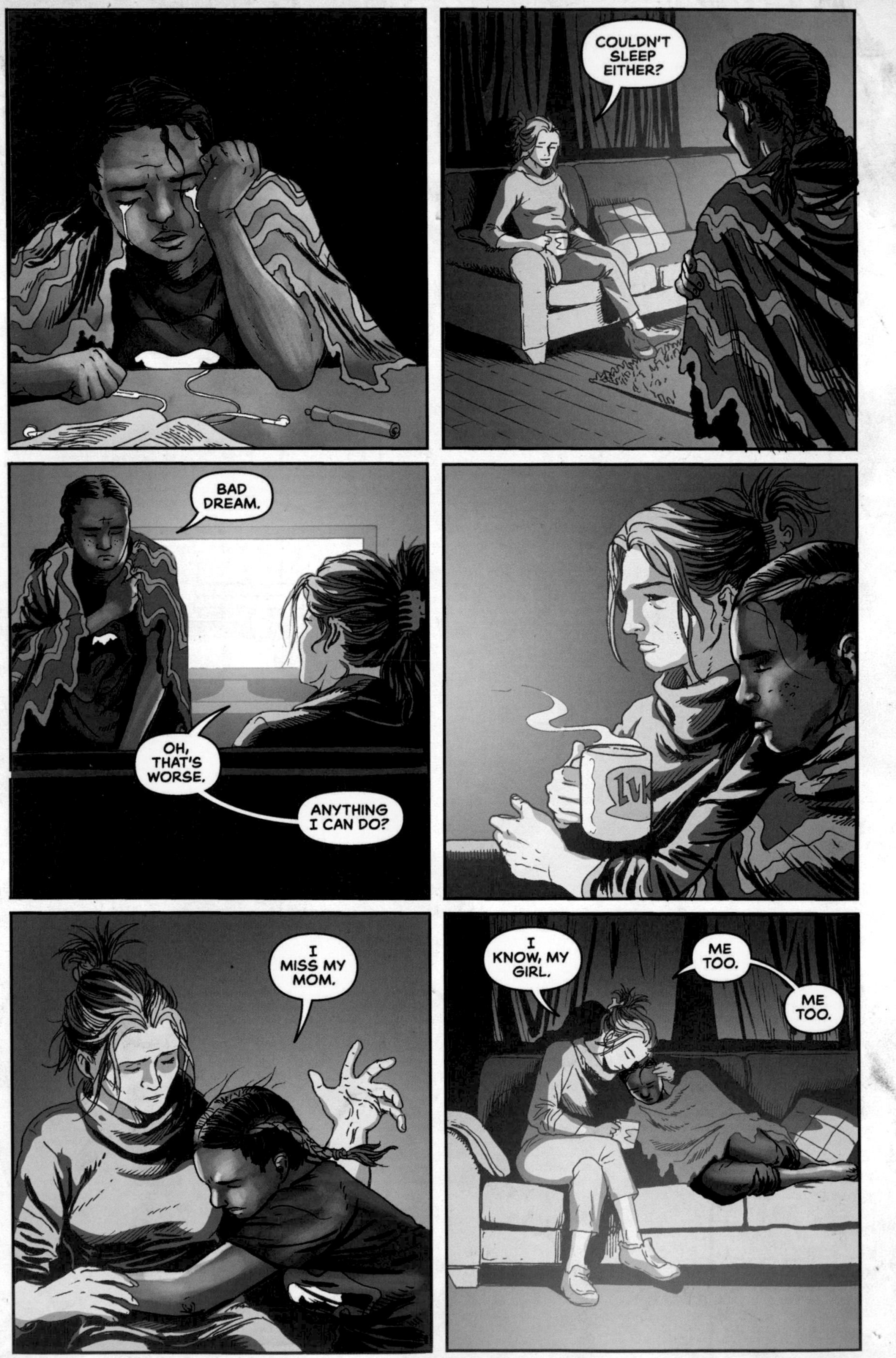
COULDN'T SLEEP EITHER?
BAD DREAM.
OH, THAT'S WORSE.
ANYTHING I CAN DO?
I MISS MY MOM.
I KNOW, MY GIRL.
ME TOO.
ME TOO.

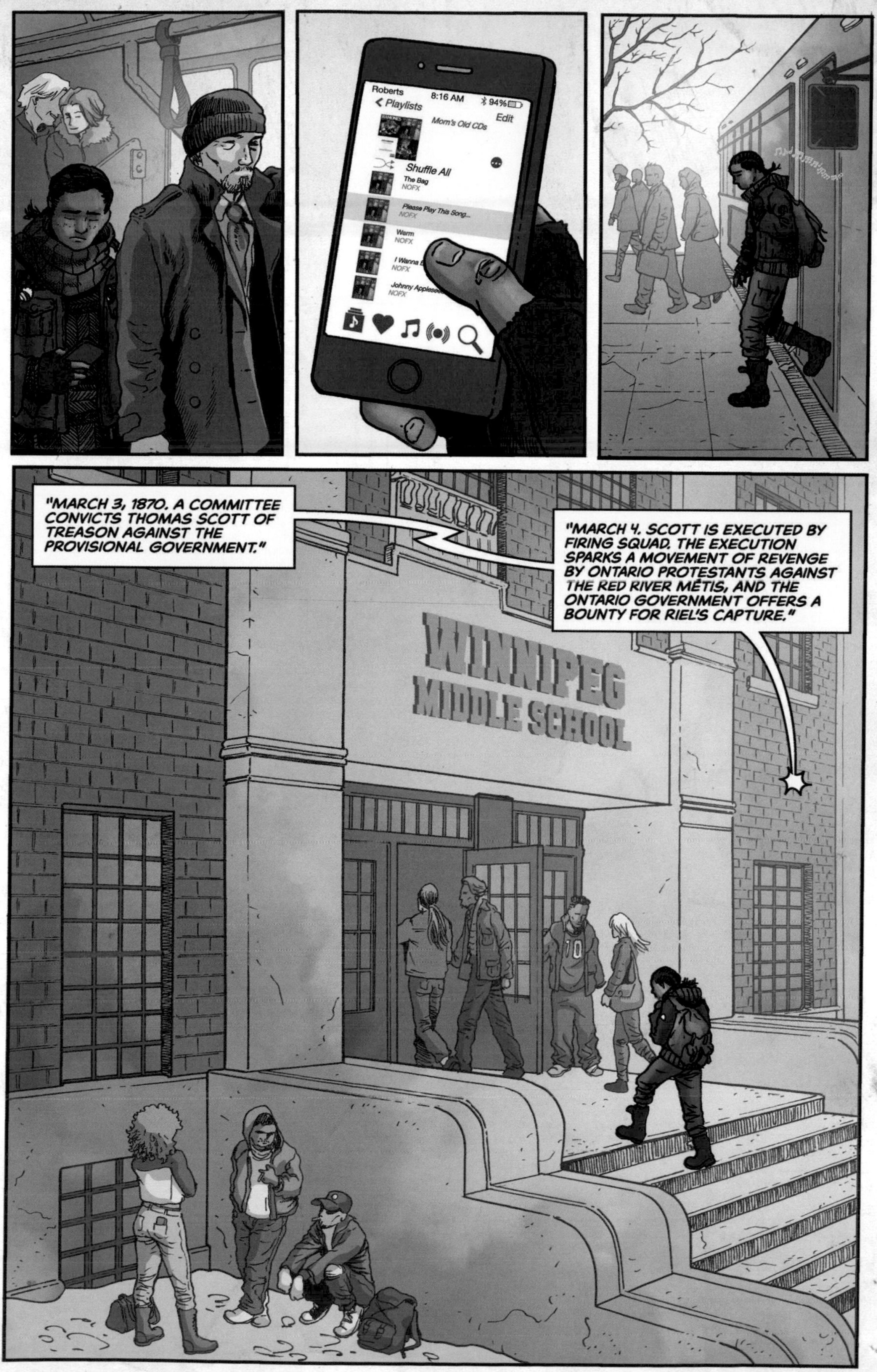
Roberts
8:16 AM
94%
Playlists
Edit
Mom's Old CDs
Shuffle All
The Bag
NOFX
Please Play This Song...
NOFX
Warm
NOFX
NOFX
"MARCH 3, 1870. A COMMITTEE CONVICTS THOMAS SCOTT OF TREASON AGAINST THE PROVISIONAL GOVERNMENT."
"MARCH 4. SCOTT IS EXECUTED BY FIRING SQUAD. THE EXECUTION SPARKS A MOVEMENT OF REVENGE BY ONTARIO PROTESTANTS AGAINST THE RED RIVER MÉTIS, AND THE ONTARIO GOVERNMENT OFFERS A BOUNTY FOR RIEL'S CAPTURE."
WINNIPEG
MIDDLE SCHOOL
10

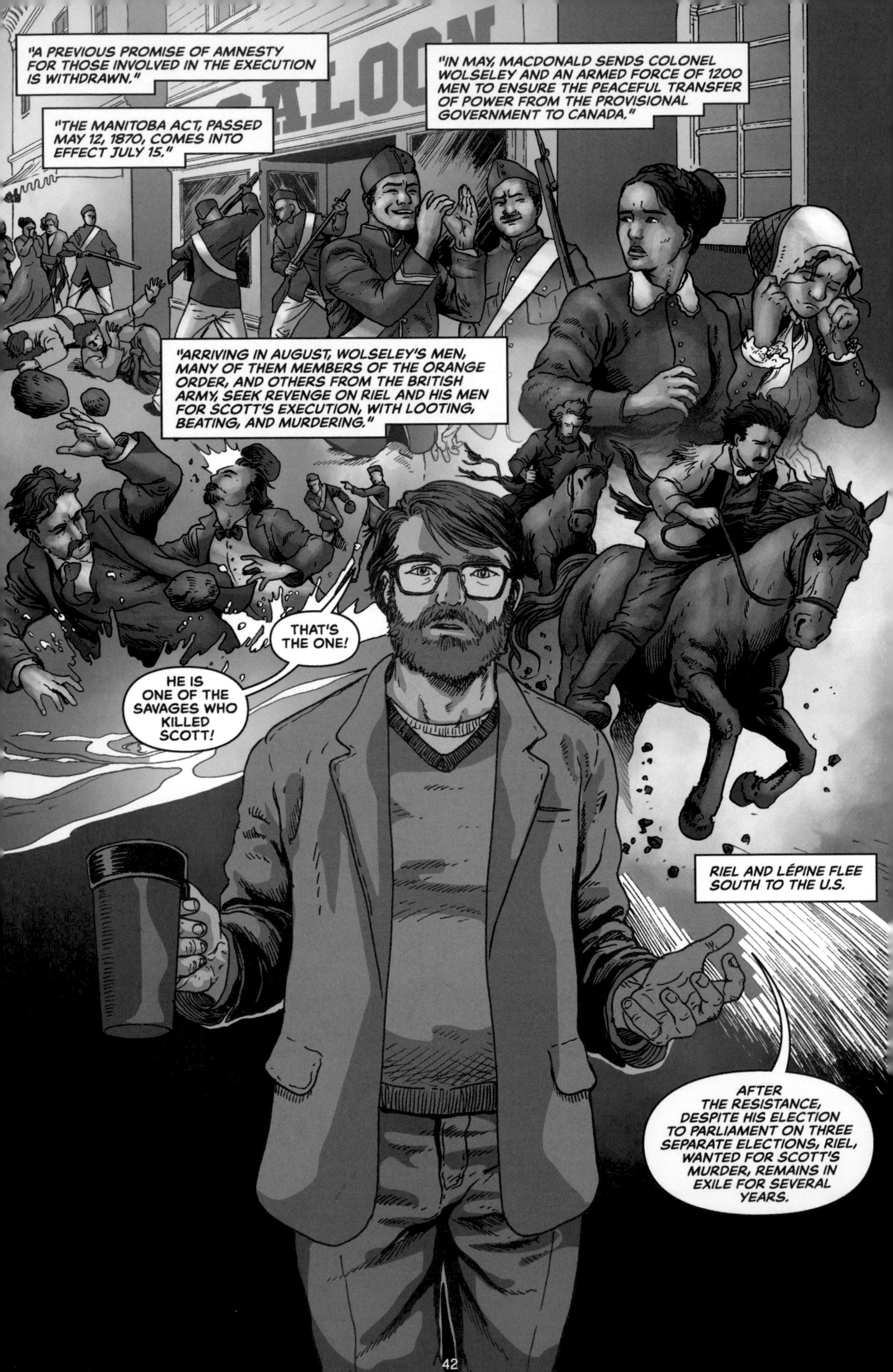
SALOON
"A PREVIOUS PROMISE OF AMNESTY FOR THOSE INVOLVED IN THE EXECUTION IS WITHDRAWN."
"THE MANITOBA ACT, PASSED MAY 12, 1870, COMES INTO EFFECT JULY 15."
"IN MAY, MACDONALD SENDS COLONEL WOLSELEY AND AN ARMED FORCE OF 1200 MEN TO ENSURE THE PEACEFUL TRANSFER OF POWER FROM THE PROVISIONAL GOVERNMENT TO CANADA."
"ARRIVING IN AUGUST, WOLSELEY'S MEN, MANY OF THEM MEMBERS OF THE ORANGE ORDER, AND OTHERS FROM THE BRITISH ARMY, SEEK REVENGE ON RIEL AND HIS MEN FOR SCOTT'S EXECUTION, WITH LOOTING, BEATING, AND MURDERING."
THAT'S THE ONE!
HE IS ONE OF THE SAVAGES WHO KILLED SCOTT!
RIEL AND LÉPINE FLEE SOUTH TO THE U.S.
AFTER THE RESISTANCE, DESPITE HIS ELECTION TO PARLIAMENT ON THREE SEPARATE ELECTIONS, RIEL, WANTED FOR SCOTT'S MURDER, REMAINS IN EXILE FOR SEVERAL YEARS.

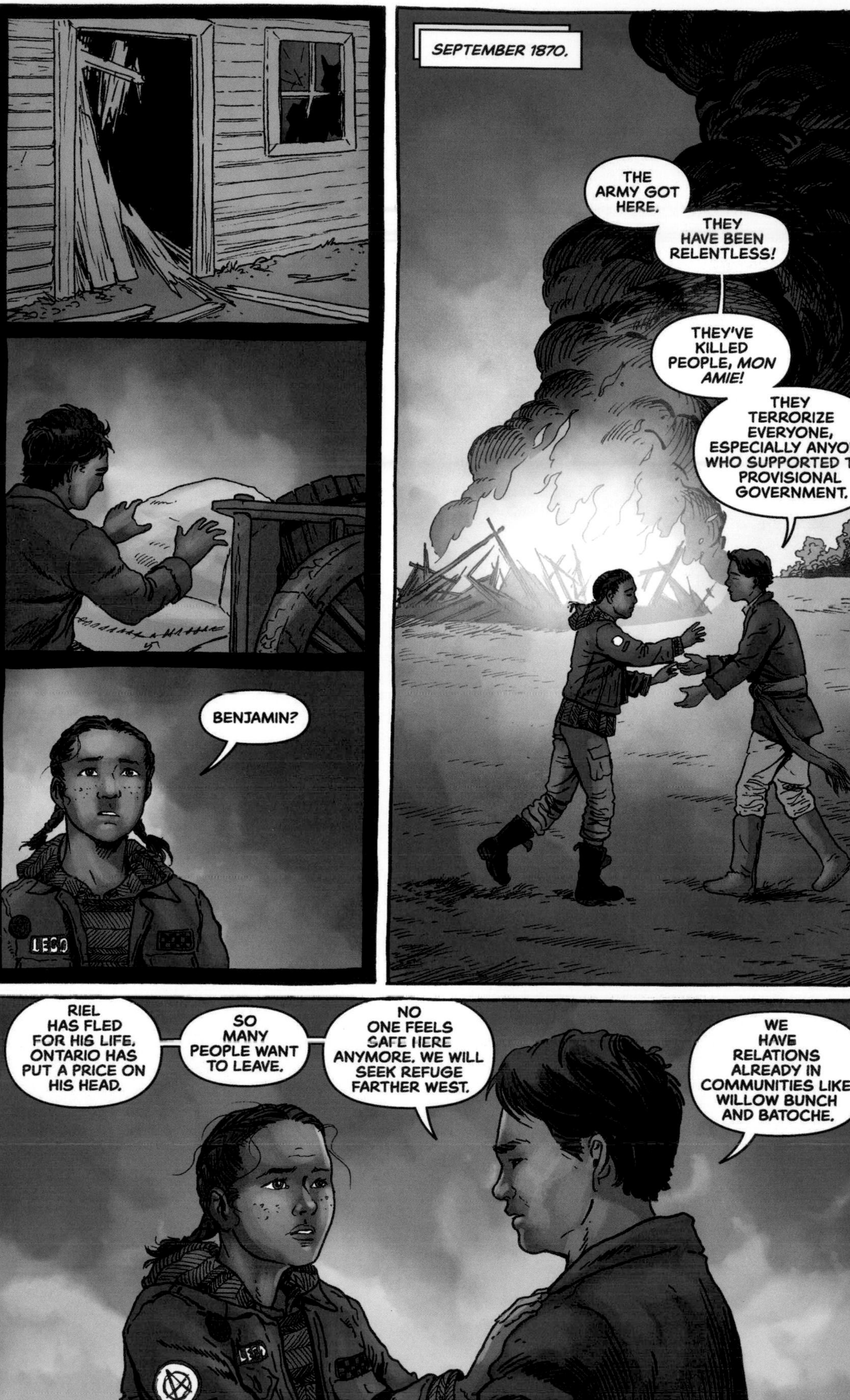
BENJAMIN?
SEPTEMBER 1870.
THE ARMY GOT HERE.
THEY HAVE BEEN RELENTLESS!
THEY'VE KILLED PEOPLE, MON AMIE!
THEY TERRORIZE EVERYONE, ESPECIALLY ANYONE WHO SUPPORTED THE PROVISIONAL GOVERNMENT.
RIEL HAS FLED FOR HIS LIFE. ONTARIO HAS PUT A PRICE ON HIS HEAD.
SO MANY PEOPLE WANT TO LEAVE.
NO ONE FEELS SAFE HERE ANYMORE. WE WILL SEEK REFUGE FARTHER WEST.
WE HAVE RELATIONS ALREADY IN COMMUNITIES LIKE WILLOW BUNCH AND BATOCHE.

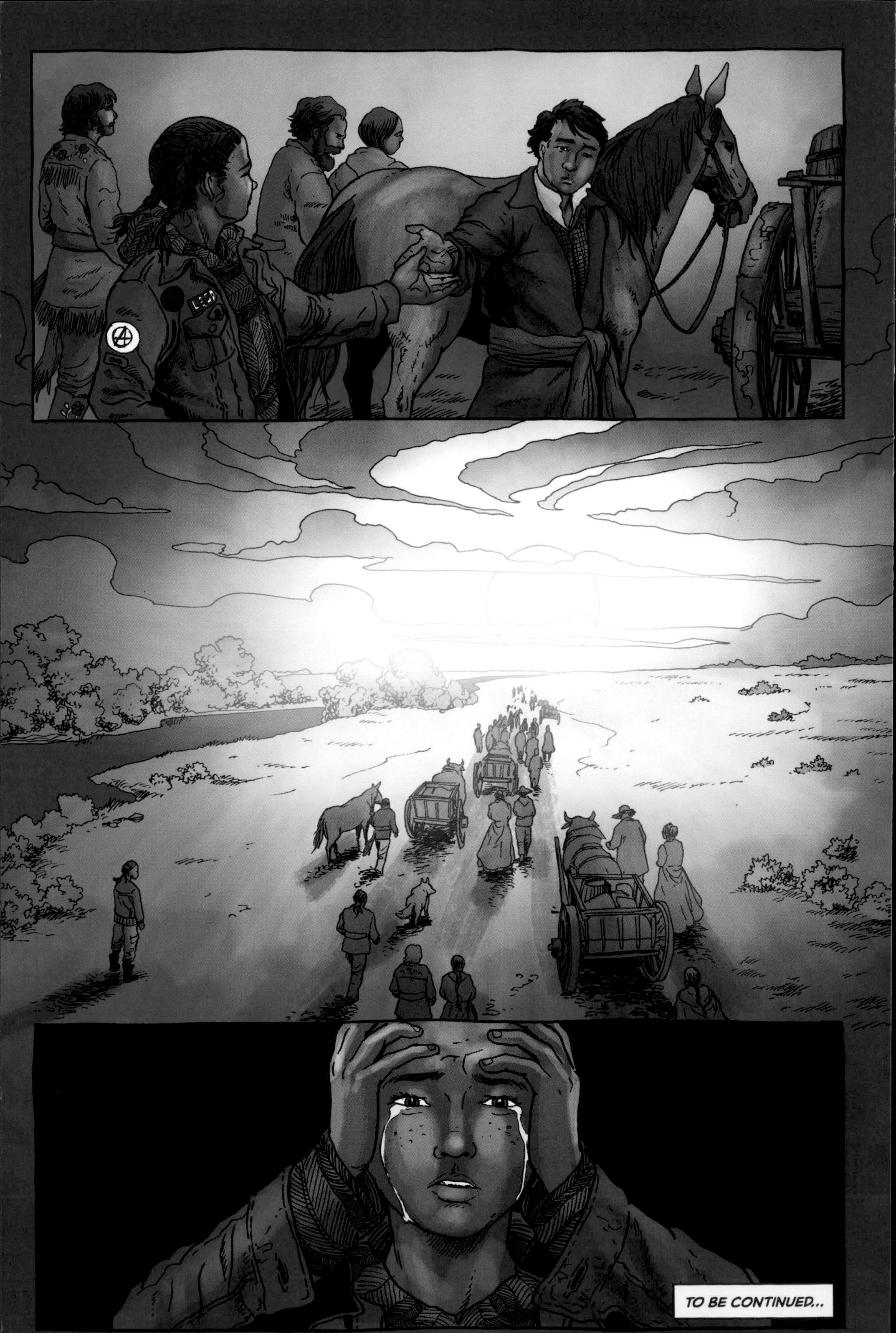
TO BE CONTINUED...

TIMELINE OF THE
RED RIVER RESISTANCE

Throughout the 1860s, immigrants from Canada started arriving in Red River Colony. Some came to farm; others came as land speculators. Many were members of the Canada First movement, which promoted the annexation of Red River by the Canadian government and encouraged Anglo-Protestant immigration from Ontario. The Métis were suspicious of their ambitions and wanted to be involved in any negotiations with Canada.

Oct. 22, 1844 – Louis Riel is born in the Red River Settlement to Louis Riel Sr. and Julie Lagimodière.

1858 – Riel is sent to Lower Canada to be trained for the priesthood.

1864 – Riel leaves school to work as a law clerk to support his family following his father's death.

1868 – Riel returns to Red River.

1869

July 19 – Riel addresses a gathering of Métis residents about the Canadian government's plans to annex Hudson's Bay Company (HBC) lands and about their rights as original inhabitants.

October 11 – Andre Nault spies a Canadian survey party on a neighbour's land. Riel and a group of Métis turn the surveyors away.

October 25 – Riel tells the HBC's Council of Assiniboia that lieutenant governor William McDougall will be barred entry into the Red River Colony until terms are negotiated between the Métis and Canadian government.

November 2 – A group of Métis, led by Ambroise Lépine, block McDougall from entering Red River and send him back to the U.S. On the same day, the committee takes over Fort Garry, administrative headquarters of the Red River settlement.

December 1 – Though the official transfer of land to Canada had been set for this date, Sir John A. Macdonald postpones payment to the HBC until the troubles are resolved. McDougall, in Pembina, unaware that the transfer had been held up, issues his own proclamation of the transfer of Assiniboia to Canada.

December 7 – A group of Canadians who plan to attack the fort barricade themselves in John Schultz's home. They are captured by Riel's men and imprisoned. Schultz is leader of the Canada First movement.

December 8 – The National Committee of the Métis forms a Provisional Government to negotiate terms of a union with Canada. The government includes both French and English inhabitants of the settlement.

December 10 – The Provisional Government raises its flag at Upper Fort Garry to show its authority in the territory.

December 27 – Riel is elected president of the Provisional Government. Donald Smith, Canadian government envoy, arrives.

1870

January 9 – Charles Mair and Thomas Scott, Canada Firsters, escape from prison.

January 19 – More than 1000 people attend a public meeting with Smith and Riel. Riel announces the election of the Convention of 40 (20 French, 20 English), to complete the list of rights and negotiate with Canada.

January 23 – John Schultz escapes from prison. He plans to overthrow the Métis.

February 3 – Métis List of Rights is adopted to be the basis of negotiations with Canada.

February 10 – The Convention of 40 is dissolved. A council of 24 delegates is elected from the parishes with four more from Winnipeg.

February 12 – The Provisional Government frees the remaining prisoners, with the proviso that they not interfere with the Government's work.

February 15 – Norbert Parisien, an intellectually delayed Métis labourer, is taken into custody as a spy by Schultz and his men in Kildonan. The following day, Parisien, frightened for his life, tries to escape. He shoots a man, Hugh Sutherland, and is beaten by a mob headed by Thomas Scott. On March 4, he succumbs to his injuries and dies.

February 17 – Forty-eight Canada Firsters, among them Thomas Scott, are arrested by Riel's men. The abusive Scott threatens his captors, and has to be isolated and restrained.

March 3 – Thomas Scott is brought before the Provisional Government court. He is found guilty of defying government authority, fighting with the guards, and insulting the president. He is sentenced to death.

March 4 – Scott is executed by firing squad. This makes him a martyr in Ontario, heightening opposition to the Red River cause.

March 8 – Bishop Taché returns to Red River as an emissary of the Canadian government, with a promise of amnesty for those in the Provisional Government.

March 9 – The Legislative Assembly of Assiniboia (LAA) is formed and operates until June 24, 1870.

March 15 – The prisoners are released on a promise of peace.

April 25 to May 2 – Manitoba delegates Father Noël Joseph Ritchot, Alfred Scott, and Judge John Black arrive in Ottawa and negotiate terms of Confederation with the Canadian government.

May 12 – The Manitoba Act, based on the final Métis List of Rights, is passed by the Canadian Parliament, to make Manitoba Canada's fifth province.

June 23 – The Legislative Assembly of Assiniboia meets to receive the report of their delegates to Ottawa. The next day, it unanimously approves entry into confederation via acceptance of the terms of the Manitoba Act.

August 24 – The Wolseley expedition, a military force sent to oversee the transfer from the Provisional Government to Canada, arrives. They take command of Upper Fort Garry, recently vacated by Riel and his followers.

Aftermath: Anti-Métis sentiment whipped up by Schultz and his men, as well as outrage at the execution of Thomas Scott, found sympathy among the military force. Many soldiers sought to avenge the death of Scott, and Riel, fearing for his life, fled for the U.S. accompanied by Ambroise Lépine.

The reign of terror against Métis and Indigenous residents lasted for years, compelling many to flee west.

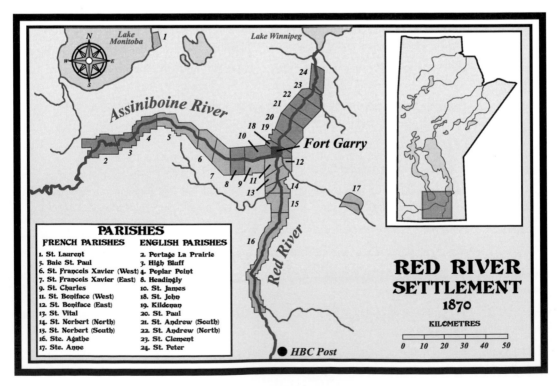

Lake Monitoba
N
E
S
W
Lake Winnipeg
Assiniboine River
Fort Garry
Red River
HBC Post
1 2 3 4 5 6 7 8 9 10 11 12 13 14 15 16 17 18 19 20 21 22 23 24
PARISHES
FRENCH PARISHES
1. St. Laurent
5. Baie St. Paul
6. St. Francois Xavier (West)
7. St. Francois Xavier (East)
9. St. Charles
11. St. Boniface (West)
12. St. Boniface (East)
13. St. Vital
14. St. Norbert (North)
15. St. Norbert (South)
16. Ste. Agathe
17. Ste. Anne
ENGLISH PARISHES
2. Portage La Prairie
3. High Bluff
4. Poplar Point
8. Headingly
10. St. James
18. St. John
19. Kildonan
20. St. Paul
21. St. Andrew (South)
22. St. Andrew (North)
23. St. Clement
24. St. Peter
RED RIVER
SETTLEMENT
1870
KILOMETRES
0 10 20 30 40 50

MÉTIS LIST OF RIGHTS
May 9, 1870

1. That this province be governed:
   a. By a Lieutenant-Governor, appointed by the Governor-General of Canada;
   b. By a Senate;
   c. By a Legislature chosen by the people with a responsible ministry.

2. That, until such time as the increase of the population in this country entitle us to a greater number, we have two representatives in the Senate and four in the Commons of Canada.

3. That in entering the Confederation the Province of the Northwest be completely free from the public debt of Canada; and if called upon to assume a part of the said debt of Canada, that it be only after having received from Canada the same amount for which the said Province of the Northwest should be held responsible.

4. That the annual sum of $80,000 be allotted by the Dominion of Canada to the Legislature of the Province of the Northwest.

5. That all properties, rights and privileges enjoyed by us up to this day be respected, and that the recognition and settlement of customs, usages and privileges be left exclusively to the decision of the Local Legislature.

6. That this country be submitted to no direct taxation except such as may be imposed by the local legislature for municipal or other local purposes.

7. That the schools be separate, and that the public money for schools be distributed among the different religious denominations in proportion to their respective populations according to the system of the Province of Quebec.

8. That the determination of the qualifications of members for the parliament of the province or for the parliament of Canada be left to the local legislature.

9. That in this province, with the exception of the Indians, who are neither civilized nor settled, every man having attained the age of 21 years, and every foreigner being a British subject, after having resided three years in this country, and being Possessed of a house, be entitled to vote at the elections for the members of the local legislature and of the Canadian Parliament, and that every foreigner other than a British subject, having resided here during the same period, and being proprietor of a house, be likewise entitled to vote on condition of taking the oath of allegiance. It is understood that this article is subject to amendment, by the local legislature exclusively.

10. That the bargain of the Hudson Bay Company with respect to the transfer of government of this country to the Dominion of Canada, never have in any case an effect prejudicial to the rights of Northwest.

11. That the Local Legislature of this Province have full control over all the lands of the Northwest.

12. That a commission of engineers appointed by Canada explore the various districts of the Northwest, and lay before the Local Legislature within the space of five years a report of the mineral wealth of the country.

13. That treaties be concluded between Canada and the different Indian tribes of the Northwest, at the request and with the co-operation of the Local Legislature.

14. That an uninterrupted steam communication from Lake Superior to Fort Garry be guaranteed to be completed within the space of five years, as well as the construction of a railroad connecting the American railway as soon as the latter reaches the international boundary.

15. That all public buildings and constructions be at the cost of the Canadian Exchequer.

16. That both the English and French languages be common in the Legislature and in the Courts; and that all public documents as well as the acts of the Legislature be published in both languages.

17. That the Lieutenant-Governor to be appointed for the province of the Northwest be familiar with both the English and French languages.

18. That the Judge of the Supreme Court speak the English and French languages.

19. That all debts contracted by the Provisional government of the territory of the Northwest, now called Assiniboia, in consequence of the illegal and inconsiderate measures adopted by Canadian officials to bring about a civil war in our midst, be paid out of the Dominion treasury, and that none of the Provisional government, or any of those acting under them, be in any way held liable or responsible with regard to the movement or any of the actions which led to the present negotiations.

© 2018 Katherena Vermette (text)
© 2018 Scott Henderson (illustration)

Excerpts from this publication may be reproduced under licence from Access Copyright, or with the express written permission of HighWater Press, or as permitted by law.

All rights are otherwise reserved, and no part of this publication may be reproduced, stored in a retrieval system, or transmitted in any form or by any means—electronic, mechanical, photocopying, scanning, recording, or otherwise—except as specifically authorized.

 Canada Council   Conseil des Arts
for the Arts   du Canada

We acknowledge the support of the Canada Council for the Arts.
Nous remercions le Conseil des arts du Canada de son soutien.

HighWater Press gratefully acknowledges the financial support of the Province of Manitoba through the Department of Sport, Culture and Heritage and the Manitoba Book Publishing Tax Credit, and the Government of Canada through the Canada Book Fund (CBF) for our publishing activities.

HighWater Press is an imprint of Portage & Main Press.
Printed and bound in Canada by Friesens
Design by Relish New Brand Experience
Content reviewer: Lawrence Barkwell, Coordinator of Metis Heritage and History Research,
                   Louis Riel Institute

For the second printing, the author corrected a date in the first panel on page 37.

Library and Archives Canada Cataloguing in Publication

Vermette, Katherena, 1977-, author
        Red River resistance / by Katherena Vermette ; illustrated by Scott B.
Henderson ; colour art by Donovan Yaciuk.

(A girl called Echo ; vol. 2)
Issued in print and electronic formats.
ISBN 978-1-55379-747-0 (softcover).--ISBN 978-1-55379-765-4 (EPUB).--
ISBN 978-1-55379-766-1 (PDF)

        I. Graphic novels. I. Henderson, Scott B., illustrator II. Yaciuk,
Donovan, 1975-, colourist III. Title. IV. Series: Vermette, Katherena,
1977- . Girl called Echo ; v. 2.

PN6733.V47R43 2018   j741.5'971   C2018-904673-2
                                               C2018-904674-0

23 22 21 20   2 3 4 5 6

HIGHWATER
   PRESS

www.highwaterpress.com
Winnipeg, Manitoba
Treaty 1 Territory and homeland of the Métis Nation